"Tell me what it is you want from me,"

Caleb said softly.

"You won't like it," Victoria confided. "I thought I might try to act like some of the women you date, catch you off guard, convince you."

"Convince me to do what?"

Victoria shook her head.

"Oh, I'm clearly no good with this seduction business. The fact that I even thought of trying is just one more example of how desperate I've become."

"You're desperate?" he asked gently, and somehow he was taking her by the arms and walking her backward slowly, easing her onto a couch. He sat beside her and she nearly jumped out of her skin. "Victoria," he said. "Tell me what's wrong."

She couldn't help it. Looking into his eyes, she couldn't seem to think clearly, to choose her words wisely. She had never been any good at playing. Blunt and truthful had always been her way.

"I want you to give me a baby."

Dear Reader,

Let this month's collection of Silhouette Romance books sweep you into the poetry of love!

Roses are red,
or white in the case of these *Nighttime Sweethearts* (SR #1754) by Cara Colter. Scarred both physically and emotionally, this cynical architect will only woo his long-lost love under the protection of night. Can a bright beauty tame this dark beast? Find out in the fourth title of Silhouette Romance's exquisite IN A FAIRY TALE WORLD… miniseries.

Violets are blue,
like the eyes of the ladies' man in Myrna Mackenzie's latest, *Instant Marriage, Just Add Groom* (SR #1755). All business, even in his relationships, this hardened hero would never father a child without the protection of marriage—but he didn't count on falling for the prim bookseller next door!

Cupid's at play,
and he's got the use of more than arrows for matchmaking! Even a blinding blizzard can bring two reluctant people together. Watch the steam rise when a gruff, reclusive writer is stranded with a single mom and her adorable baby in *Daddy, He Wrote* (SR #1756) by Jill Limber.

And magic, too!
With only six days left to break her curse, Cat knew she couldn't count on finding true love. Until she happened upon a dark, reticent veterinarian with a penchant for rescuing animals—and damsels—in distress! You're sure to be enchanted by Shirley Jump's SOULMATES story, *Kissed by Cat* (SR #1757).

May love find *you* this Valentine's Day!
Mavis C. Allen
Associate Senior Editor

Please address questions and book requests to:
Silhouette Reader Service
U.S.: 3010 Walden Ave., P.O. Box 1325, Buffalo, NY 14269
Canadian: P.O. Box 609, Fort Erie, Ont. L2A 5X3

Instant Marriage, Just Add Groom

MYRNA MACKENZIE

SILHOUETTE *Romance*®

Published by Silhouette Books

America's Publisher of Contemporary Romance

SILHOUETTE BOOKS

ISBN 0-373-19755-1

INSTANT MARRIAGE, JUST ADD GROOM

Visit Silhouette Books at www.eHarlequin.com

Printed in U.S.A.

MYRNA MACKENZIE,

is the winner of the Holt Medallion honoring outstanding fiction and a finalist for numerous other awards including the Orange Rose, the National Readers' Choice Award, the *Romantic Times* Reviewer's Choice and Wis RWA's Write Touch. She believes that humor, love and hope are three of the best medicines in the world and tries to make sure that her books reflect that belief. Born in a small town in southern Missouri, Myrna grew up in the Chicago area, married her high school sweetheart and has two teenage sons. Her hobbies include dreaming of warmer climes during the cold northern winters, pretending the dust in her house doesn't exist, taking long walks and traveling. Readers can write to Myrna at P.O. Box 225, LaGrange, IL 60525, or they may visit her online at www.myrnamackenzie.com.

WANTED:

A virile man of intelligence and good character to father a child. Will pay up front. No future commitments once the goal is accomplished. Must supply five character references and three business references. Send responses to Future Mom.

Chapter One

"Thirty-six isn't so old," Victoria Holbrook muttered to herself as she walked toward home after closing up her bookshop. Thirty-six still left plenty of time to do things.

"Oh, hello, hello, Miss Holbrook. Look. Look. Look," six-year-old Misty Ordway called. "I got a brand-new baby." The little girl skipped down the dusty street toward Victoria, dragging her baby doll by one arm. Misty's blue eyes were round with excitement, and Victoria couldn't help smiling.

"She's a very pretty baby, too," Victoria said, but as Misty flew past, Victoria was thinking, *If I had gotten married and gotten pregnant when I was twenty-nine, I might have had my own Misty by now.*

But she hadn't. She hadn't even come close. Sadly, she watched Misty continue down the street, talking to her "baby."

"How's it going, Victoria?" Flora Ellers asked as Victoria passed the local fruit market that Flora and her husband owned. Flora shifted her very real baby, twelve-month-old Sammy, to one hip, and he cooed and patted at her with a tiny chubby hand. Flora responded to his gesture by kissing his sweet little forehead.

Victoria's heart clenched. "It's going quite well, Flora. Thank you for asking. I hope you're well, too," she said, but even though Flora was a dear and she looked as if she might want to chat, Victoria excused herself as she hurried away in the direction of her house. Still, no matter how easily she could run away from her neighbors and the painful outward reminders of her own failure to conceive by the age she had set herself years ago, there was no running away from the actual truth.

"It" was not going quite well, not well at all, in fact. Today she was thirty-six years old. Next year at this time she would be thirty-seven and then thirty-eight and thirty-nine. In no time at all, her ovaries and everything that made her fertile would start the process of shutting down, incorrectly assuming that she was done with childbearing.

"Why, I haven't even started," Victoria murmured, just as she felt the breeze of a large body brushing past hers.

"Excuse me. Started what?"

Victoria shook her head and, startled, glanced up, right into the silver-blue eyes of Caleb Fremont, the much-too-handsome owner of the Renewal, Illinois, *Gazette*. She blinked and tried to get her bearings.

Caleb Fremont frowned, and she realized what a large man he was. She had never actually been this close to him before. In fact, in the two years since she had moved to Renewal, she had never really talked to the man, outside of a formal introduction at a business association meeting when she had first come here. He was staring at her now as if waiting for her to speak. She supposed that was what he was waiting for, since she hadn't answered his question.

"Are you all right, Ms. Holbrook?" he asked gently. "It *is* Ms. Holbrook, isn't it?"

Hmm, Renewal wasn't a particularly large town, and the man dealt in names and facts, yet he couldn't completely connect her with her name? Victoria felt her spirits drop even more. Not that it was terribly surprising that she was still a mystery to some of the townspeople. She *did* tend to keep to herself. She ran a bookstore that dealt primarily in historical tomes. Not exactly Caleb Fremont's cup of tea, she would wager. He was dedicated to his newspaper, but he was also a man with a busy social life. And sometimes that social life included women. At least according to gossip, it included the women from the neighboring towns. She doubted that he spent his evenings reading historical works to them.

"I—yes, I'm fine," she said, as embarrassment crept in. But she refused to let it show. She had never been the type who displayed her emotions. It just wasn't in her nature. In fact, the very thought of letting anyone see inside her was horrifying. She remembered all too well how that had perplexed her parents. They had run a small dinner theater. The most loving, open, gregarious people in the world, they had had this terrifying habit of spilling all their secrets—and hers—to anyone who happened to cross their paths. Victoria had faced that humiliation many times before she learned not to share anything, a fact that bewildered and hurt her heart-on-their-sleeves parents.

"Ms. Holbrook?"

Victoria mentally shook herself.

"I'm sorry," she said, regaining her carefully controlled expression. "Actually, I'm totally all right, Mr. Fremont. I was just thinking about my business, and I guess the words just slipped out." She felt a tiny nip of guilt at the lie, but the truth would have been so much worse. To let the town's most notorious bachelor realize that she was fretting about the fact that she might never have a child? That the reason she might never have a child was due to the fact that she had never even been intimately involved with a man? Especially when this man probably climbed into bed with women on a daily basis? Impossible.

"Are you sure that you're all right, Ms. Holbrook? Forgive me for saying so, but you're looking a bit anxious."

Victoria blinked. She knew that if she stared into a mirror, she would see what everyone else saw every day, a calm, cool, very plain woman dressed in black and white. No trace of color, no trace of emotion, no telltale signs of her distress, which was, of course, just the way she liked things. How could Caleb Fremont have even begun to suspect that she was concerned about anything? Drat the reporter in him. She wondered if he gazed at the women he dated and read their souls.

Silly thought. Of course he didn't. He probably didn't

look even slightly beyond their long blond or black or red hair and their red lips and plump breasts as he undressed them. Wasn't that what Caleb Fremont was reputed to be about, anyway, when he wasn't publishing the newspaper? With that chestnut hair and those silver-blue eyes, he had the ladies of Renewal sighing whenever he walked by. He probably saw women only as bed partners, just bodies. Of course, she could tell by the way he was looking at her, that he had no interest in the body beneath her loose clothing.

And suddenly, thinking of Caleb Fremont and these completely improper thoughts, Victoria became aware of her own body in quite a distinct way. Her breasts felt tight, her skin too sensitive. She cursed her own weakness and shifted in an attempt to rid herself of the sensations.

"Maybe you should sit down, Ms. Holbrook," Caleb suggested, motioning toward one of the random benches the town council had placed on the streets. "Is there someone I could call for you?"

No, there was no one. She was completely on her own, and she was apparently acting strangely, so strangely that a man who barely even knew she existed had noted that she was acting out of character. That just wouldn't do.

Shoving her crazy feelings away, Victoria managed a tight smile. "I'm sorry, Mr. Fremont, but I'm really quite fine. Just put my unusual demeanor down to another birthday come and almost gone. I'm afraid I was assessing my accomplishments and finding that I had fallen down on the job in some respects."

Caleb arched a chestnut brow. "I find that hard to believe, Ms. Holbrook. The townspeople speak quite highly of you, you know. That bookseller's award they gave you is just an example. When you brought the first bookstore to Renewal two years ago, it was big news for the town."

"Maybe, but I don't think Timeless Publications was exactly what anyone expected. No fiction, no magazines, no children's books and I do most of my business via the Internet. I'm not sure that would be considered an accomplishment by most people."

Caleb shrugged, his broad shoulders emphasizing the lean lines of the rest of his body. His tie had been pushed aside now that the day was over, and a trace of crisp chest hair showed at the V of his white shirt.

Victoria felt another curious lurch inside her body. For a second she wondered about those women he was reputed to date and she quickly looked away. Certainly she didn't want to waste her time wondering what Caleb Fremont's "type" was and whether she met his criteria. Who could tell anyway? None of the women in Renewal, apparently, suited him. Caleb, she had heard, had a strict rule about dating the women of the town he lived in.

"Your bookstore might not have been all that everyone expected," he said, "but it did bring a boost to the town's economy in that other stores followed. We're getting quite a reputation as the town that books built."

If she were a blushing woman, she would have blushed with pride. As it was, she hid the foolish sense of warmth that spread through her at Caleb's compliment. Most people didn't make the connection between her store and the other new merchants. Somehow she managed an awkward thank you. "And really, Mr. Fremont, you needn't be concerned about me at all. I'm just on my way home. I was woolgathering, but that's not unusual for a woman who deals in books."

He nodded, the late-afternoon sunlight catching the glint of gold in his hair. "All right, then. Happy birthday, Ms. Holbrook. I hope you have a very fine day. A birthday should be special."

Yes, it should be, Victoria acknowledged as the most handsome man in town walked away from her. But her birthdays were simply becoming distressing, not special. They were making her act strange and feel even more strange, the way she had been these past few minutes. Her birthdays had become markers proclaiming that she was not a young woman anymore, that she was getting older by the second and that she was nowhere near to achieving her goals. If she continued as she had been, she never would get what she wanted.

Time was running away from her in a mad rush, faster and faster, and so far she had simply stood by and let that happen, which wasn't her way at all. She was quiet, but by nature she was a doer. So what was she going to do about her baby problem?

Victoria continued on her way. "Something," she whispered. "I think I'm going to have to do something drastic." Something terribly out of character.

She wondered when she would do it. More than that, she wondered what it was she was going to do.

* * *

"Did you see what Victoria Holbrook is doing?"

Caleb looked up at his assistant, Denise, who was shaking her head and clucking. Denise was an efficient and talented assistant. Unfortunately, she was also a world-class gossip. She seemed to think that working for a newspaper necessitated her spying on all of the people of Renewal.

Caleb thought of the wistful expression he had witnessed in Victoria Holbrook's eyes last night. Although she had come to Renewal two years ago, he didn't really know anything about her at all. They traveled in completely different circles, or at least he traveled in circles. She seemed to be a very private person, which was something he could certainly understand. So, ignoring Denise's question, Caleb continued working.

"She's painting the sign over her business, that's what she's doing. It's been stark black and white for two years, and now she's painting it royal blue and gold. I wonder why."

Caleb gave up ignoring Denise. "Maybe she likes royal blue and gold."

Denise gave him a look that would have killed lesser men, but Caleb didn't even flinch. Still, she frowned and tapped her foot on the ground, until he was afraid she might inflate and explode right there in front of him. A messy business that would be. What's more, she probably wouldn't be any help at all in getting the next edition of the paper out if he didn't humor her just a touch. "All right, Denise," Caleb finally said, crossing his arms and leaning back in his chair. "Just why do you think Victoria Holbrook is painting her sign?"

"Middle-age crisis," Denise said with conviction. "It's so obvious. It's so sad."

Caleb only stared.

"She's getting older, hon," Denise explained patiently. "And she doesn't like it."

Caleb remembered that Victoria's chin-length plain brown hair hadn't held a trace of gray, which probably didn't mean much. But her eyes had been clear, her complexion fair and smooth, and that did mean something. "She doesn't look that old to me."

"Oh, really? Just when did you start noticing how the women in this town looked? I thought you stayed away from Renewal women."

Caleb shrugged nonchalantly. "I don't date Renewal women, but I have eyes, and they work just fine."

His assistant smiled triumphantly. "So you look, but you just don't touch. At least, you don't touch your neighbors."

He frowned at her. He knew that everyone, including Denise, thought he was a grade-A womanizer. Well, the truth fell somewhat short of that. He *did* date women from adjacent towns now and then, but not nearly as often as people thought. Sometimes he just holed up with a good book or he met with friends, but if people thought the women of Dalloway or Mornington were wearing him out, then that was okay.

Having a reputation for loving and leaving women on a weekly basis made him less desirable as a catch to the women he spent most of his days with. He was clearly, in their eyes, a poor choice for anything resembling forever, and they were right. He didn't believe in fairy tales and happy endings and love that lasted forever. He had no experience of such things, and certainly wasn't capable of that kind of deep emotional attachment. So, let everyone think that he went to Dalloway seeking debauchery every other weekend. Because that way he could indulge in his real love, this newspaper, and no one seemed to mind. Except for Denise, of course, who always seemed personally offended that he refused to settle down and get married to one of Renewal's fine ladies.

"You would never in this lifetime consider hooking up with a woman who lived here. Isn't that right, Caleb?" she asked again.

He gave her a look that told her she had crossed the line. She ignored him. "You already knew that. Now do you think we could possibly get this paper out the door?"

"Don't worry, we will. Don't we always? And don't you think it's sad?"

"What's sad?"

"Victoria Holbrook. I think it's just awful that the woman is afraid she's getting old and all she can think of to kick up her heels a little is to paint the sign on the front of her business. Don't you?"

But Caleb had had enough. "Work, Denise," he ordered. Because what he thought was that Victoria Holbrook's age and her looks and her sign were none of his business. He was a healthy, normal male, and he did healthy, normal male things on a reasonably regular basis, but the truth was that he *did* make a point of staying away from the women in Renewal. Because no matter how normal and healthy he was, he had decided early in life that he wasn't promising what he couldn't deliver, and he certainly wasn't going to let his impermanent ways cause any ugly sticky business with the women who were his colleagues and neighbors. Getting too involved with those he worked and lived with wasn't good business and it wasn't good for the community. So he did not want to spend even one more minute thinking about dark-suited, quiet, prim little Victoria Holbrook and what made her tick.

But royal blue, eh? He sincerely hoped she had kicked up her heels yesterday and that her mood had lifted.

It was purely a neighborly thought, because as he'd mentioned, Victoria Holbrook wasn't any of his concern.

Victoria stared at the newly painted sign outside her business. It was certainly…blue, wasn't it?

For a minute, she thought about calling back the painters and asking them to put it back, to return it to its safe classic black.

"How silly you are," she whispered. "It's just a sign." But it was more than that, she knew. It was an impulse, brought on by her feelings of yesterday, and she had never been impulsive. What's more, it was a change, and she had never managed change well, either. It drew attention to her store, and she had never ever liked being the center of attention. She could still remember the years of her parents insisting she be more lively and open, that she be more like they were, that she actually appear on stage with them. Worse, the memories of the awkward and humiliating attempts to remake herself to fulfill her parents' wishes, the laughing and pointing of the crowd, left Victoria cringing.

She had begged her mother and father to let her stay backstage with a book after that, and after several more disasters, they had agreed. That had been the beginning of her quiet, unassuming life, a good and useful life that had served her well. She had only considered stepping into the spotlight a few other times over the years, to try to fit someone else's idea of who and what she should be. Once, in high school, she had tried to make herself prettier in order to attract the attention of a boy she longed to have notice her. She'd tried to fit with his crowd. The result had been…disastrous. Victoria didn't even want to think about what had happened. She had avoided looking at boys for months afterward. It hadn't been her last mistake with a man, however. Victoria felt the old panic climbing through her. She blanked the humiliating memories out of her mind, but she couldn't eliminate the nagging question. After all of that, could she really be thinking of jumping through someone else's hoops again?

"But it's not the same," she whispered. "This time they're my hoops, of my making, and I'm not looking for some fairy-tale ending. This time I only need to sustain the illusion for a very short time."

The blue sign and the changes she had made inside the store were only temporary, meaningless symbols, the first steps in the very sensible plan she had come up with. She knew that her reclusive nature, her lack of color and softness kept many people at a distance. Not all, of course. There were those who liked the quiet as much as she did, and those who were just friendly to everyone. Except for her longing for a child, she really had made a very contented life for herself here in Renewal. She had made friends, even if she wasn't the type who inspired people to draw close. She had a good home and a satisfying business.

But she wanted a baby. She longed for a child, someone who could belong just to her, to whom she could give the gift of total acceptance and affection. She didn't trust a sperm bank. Who knew if anyone was monitoring the papers that the donors filled out? Who knew who those men really were? That route wasn't going to work for her, so there was only one choice remaining. She needed a man, or at least a man's essence, his DNA. And she wanted to choose the man, to know that she had picked the best possible traits for her baby.

She *would* have her baby, even if it meant bending her own rules for a while, temporarily changing her image, doing her best to be like other women, letting a man into her bed—the one location where a woman was at her most vulnerable. But this time she wouldn't be vulnerable, because this time her emotions would not be involved at all.

This would be a business transaction. But even the best business deals needed to be set up. A sale couldn't be made unless there was a motive for someone to buy.

So she needed to sell herself, to turn herself into a desirable commodity. That would involve some scene-setting.

Changing her bookstore, the place where she spent most of her time, was the first step.

The second step was finding the man, one with all the right traits. She had gotten up early this morning and started a database. She had keyed in what she knew of the men in Renewal, then typed in what she was looking for. It was an ongoing process.

"But not really." She dared to whisper the words.

There was only one man who truly met all her requirements. He was physically attractive and seemingly intelligent. He had shown concern for her. But most important of all, he was not going to make any future demands of her. None whatsoever. He definitely didn't seem to be interested in commitment, and because of that free and easy lifestyle, he didn't mix his business or his neighbors with his pleasure.

So she just hoped she could convince him that she wasn't looking for pleasure. She just wanted him to impregnate her.

Her heart jolted at the thought, and quickly the part of her that was logical and sensible and reclusive started trotting out the reasons why this was the most ridiculous scheme she had ever come up with. It was, too. She knew that. But she was beyond caring. She wanted her child. Once she had her baby, she could live her life as she always had, with her baby, her books and her solitude.

It was a risk she was willing to take. If people laughed at her efforts, so be it. She could always move and start anew elsewhere, because she had to try just this once. If she didn't, she would always regret her cowardice. She refused to let her fears prevent her from achieving her dreams.

But, as she turned, at that moment all of her thought processes stopped.

Caleb was coming down the street toward her, and she had yet to come up with a plan on how to get him to do what she wanted him to do.

Chapter Two

Victoria Holbrook was small, Caleb thought. He hadn't noted that yesterday when he had seen her on the street. But then he supposed that he'd never noticed much of anything about her. She was quiet, unassuming in her black-and-white attire, easy to pass by.

He felt a twinge of guilt at that. He had never judged a woman simply on her appearance. He valued intelligence, and he supposed a woman who ran a rather highbrow bookstore and who managed her own business had to be intelligent. Others spoke well of her. It was just…well, it was just that she almost seemed to choose to live in the background. In her prim little suits, she almost insisted that a person's gaze slide right past her…except for that something wistful in her eyes that he had noticed yesterday. That look, those eyes, made him wonder what lay beneath her little black-and-white surface. What was it really that made Victoria Holbrook tick? And why was a woman with such melting chocolate eyes and such an upstanding character living a virtual life of solitude? Surely some other man had noticed that vulnerable look and been caught in the depths of her gaze.

He almost chuckled at that. Better not let Denise hear him say things like that. She would think he'd gone soft if he was speculating about the fine brown eyes of a Renewal woman.

Caleb nodded to Victoria and started to walk on past. Then he glanced up at the sign over her door and stopped dead in his tracks.

"Incredible." It wasn't just that the sign was bright blue and gold. It was blue with gold clouds and sprays of stars and twinkling white letters that now read Timeless Publications: Books to Dream On. It was the very opposite of the stark prim exterior that had been here before.

He glanced at the petite lady in front of the store. She had her hands clasped tightly beneath her breasts. He couldn't help but notice that her knuckles were tension white. He also couldn't help noting that she really did have some amazingly lovely curves beneath her loose black suit jacket.

What the hell? Better back away from those thoughts, buddy, he told himself. To Victoria he said, "That's an impressive sign. Is this the result of some birthday resolutions?"

She gave him a frayed little smile, not much of one at all, but it was enough to let him know that she had a pretty mouth and that she was embarrassed.

"I thought it was time to make a few changes," she said. "I'm just redecorating and adding a few things. Fiction. Children's books."

"Couches," he said, peering through the window and noticing a powder-blue couch and several deep-blue easy chairs. A small table with a lace cloth and a pitcher of yellow daisies was positioned next to one chair.

"Couches," she agreed softly. "People want those things."

Her words were firm, but her voice was threaded with uncertainty. Caleb couldn't help smiling. "I suppose some do. But what do you want, Ms. Holbrook?"

She turned her head and bit her lip slightly. Her pale pink mouth turned rosy and a very male response slid through Caleb. He ignored it. "I want people to stop calling me Ms. Holbrook," she finally said. "I've been called that…oh, for years now. It sounds so old, so stuffy. And even if I am a bit stuffy and a little old, I would prefer Victoria or even some version of Victoria."

Caleb tipped his head in agreement and smiled, giving her a small formal bow. "Your wish is my command, Victoria."

She blinked and opened her eyes very wide. "Why did you say that? Or at least, why did you say that in the way you did?"

"I try to be accommodating."

Victoria looked even more nervous. Finally she took a visible breath and frowned slightly. She looked directly up into his eyes. "How accommodating?"

"Excuse me?"

"I asked you to call me Victoria and you agreed. You implied that you try to give people what they want."

"When we're talking something as simple as a name, sure I do," Caleb said with a low chuckle. "I'm positive, though, that there are plenty who would tell you that I've given them exactly the opposite of what they want when it comes to the matter of reporting what happens in this town. Not everyone wants their business made public."

She backed away a step. Okay, the lady was hiding something. Intriguing, but...

"I don't pry for the paper, Victoria. At least not unless I'm on the trail of something newsworthy. Or unless someone has committed a crime. I don't believe you've committed any, have you?"

"Not yet."

Oh, so the lady had a sense of humor. At least he hoped she was joking.

"But I am planning to do something unorthodox. I hope it isn't newsworthy."

"Want to run it by me?"

She studied him for a few seconds as if trying to decide if he could be trusted or not. Finally, she nodded, her head jerking slightly. "Actually, I do. As I mentioned, I've decided to make some changes in my life. I'm thirty-six years old, and it's time."

He opened his mouth to speak, but she held up one small hand. "Please don't patronize me by doing the polite thing and telling me that thirty-six isn't old, Mr. Fremont."

"Caleb, Victoria," he said. "I prefer Caleb."

Her self-composed attitude slipped for a second as

those big brown eyes blinked. Then she nodded tightly. "Caleb, then," she said softly. "I just don't like it when people try to patronize me." She placed one hand on her hip in what he was sure she thought was a firm and possibly intimidating gesture. He was charmed.

"I'm not patronizing you, Victoria. I'm just…waiting."

Her firm expression slipped. "For what?"

He grinned. "For you to tell me what you *do* like and also what it is you're planning to do that is so unorthodox."

She hesitated.

"You've changed your mind? You don't want my opinion?" he asked.

Slowly she shook her head. "No, I can't change my mind, but I can't ask you right now. I still have things to do, things to put in place. Would you—that is, would you mind having dinner with me at my house tonight? It's strictly business," she said, all in a rush that practically ran the words together. "That is, I am not asking you to dinner in the conventional sense, because I completely respect your decision not to get involved with Renewal women. Actually, I would never want to get involved with you, anyway."

Caleb did a double take. The woman certainly knew how to take a man down.

"That is, it's nothing about you personally," she said quickly. "I just don't want to get involved with anyone, really. Just the way you don't want to get involved."

Well, he certainly had that coming. No doubt he should be relieved. Instead, he was simply intrigued. Victoria Holbrook was asking him to dinner at her house to discuss a business proposition. She was changing her business from hard to soft, from academic to commercial. She was very aware of the passing of time, even though she still looked like a young woman.

"Is it all right, then?" she asked, and suddenly the strong, certain businesswoman was replaced by the vulnerable lady again. "Are you interested?"

To his amazement, he was. He wasn't sure why. Maybe it was because she had compared herself to him. She was a woman who had strict rules and limits, who set boundaries. She wasn't afraid to admit that, and he was sure she had been criticized for it many times.

And now she was changing her rules a bit while still maintaining those boundaries. He barely knew who she was, although she had been here for two years. A newspaperman certainly ought to know something of his readers.

Besides, she had said this was business. He was sure it was. She was obviously a woman of truth and integrity.

But if it was business, it was sure to be something interesting. He'd never seen a confident, successful woman squirm so much when discussing business.

Oh no, he wasn't going to miss this. If Victoria Holbrook was going to do something unorthodox, then he wanted to see what it was.

Of course his interest was purely business, too, he assured himself as he said yes and turned to walk away.

But when he got back to the newspaper, he turned around to stare back in her direction. Victoria had locked her hands loosely behind her back and was gazing up at her new sign. The action emphasized her slim figure.

"So what is she doing?" Denise popped out of the building and gave him one of those spill-the-beans-boss looks.

"She's fixing up her store. Nothing unusual about that."

"You're such a *man*. When a woman like that starts changing things, it means something. She's making a statement. I wonder what it is."

"Oh, that."

Denise poked him with one of her dragon-woman nails. "What do you mean, oh, that?"

He smiled. "The statement. I know what it is."

"Yeah, what is it?"

He pushed past his assistant into the office. "She's tired of being called Ms. Holbrook by everyone. She wants to be called Victoria."

"Victoria?"

"Yes, a rather lovely name, isn't it?"

"You mean she wants *you* to call her Victoria."

"Sure, she wants me to call her that. And everyone else, too."

Denise rolled her eyes. "She *says* that, but really the rest of us, we're just a ruse. She wants you. I've seen it before."

So had Caleb, and he had hated it every time he had been forced to hurt someone's feelings. But Victoria definitely didn't want him. In fact, he had the distinct impression that she didn't really even want to do business with him. Something strange was going on.

"She doesn't want me. I think I'm the last thing she wants."

He felt a twinge of regret as he said the words out loud, and he frowned.

Denise started laughing.

"What?" he demanded.

"A woman turned you down. You hit on her, and she turned you down."

"I did *not* hit on her, Denise." But a vision of pretty legs beneath a plain black skirt rose up in his mind, and a surge of lust rippled through him.

And if she lived somewhere other than here, I *might* have hit on her, he thought. He didn't say the words aloud. Denise would have let everyone, including Victoria, know inside of an hour.

He did not want Victoria Holbrook to know that there were parts of her that brought out his male instincts.

She'd probably faint if she did know.

And then he'd have to kiss her awake.

Caleb swore beneath his breath. "Denise, let's get this paper out," he growled. "Time is short." And in only a few hours, he was going to have to deal with this strange infatuation he was feeling for Victoria Holbrook.

"I cannot do this. I cannot go through with this. What on earth was I thinking when I asked him here?" Victoria muttered to herself as she peered into her closet and tried to decide what to wear.

But she knew what she had been thinking and why she was doing this. Because time was running out. She had used it all up. She had spent too many years hiding and doing things her way.

Now, if she ever wanted to have a baby, she had to make some changes, at least for a while. She had to move into society, invite people into her life, she had to make a world that would welcome the baby she was going to have.

And she *was* going to have a baby. Caleb Fremont or some other man was going to give her one. But she wanted it to be Caleb. She had read over the articles he'd written in the past year, clear evidence that he had a wonderful and lively mind. She recalled how much the business people of the town respected Caleb for his fairness and sense of justice. And she remembered that he had been kind to her the other day. He hadn't looked at her as if she were an odd duck, the way many people did. It was also obvious that he was sound of body.

No doubt he would pass on some of what made him who he was to his offspring.

"So, you have to be convincing, Victoria. You have to be a saleswoman, and above all you have to convince him that you want nothing from him beyond what is necessary to produce a child."

Victoria shivered at the thought of what was "necessary." She was pretty sure that Caleb was pretty good at doing *that*.

"Not that it matters," she said, looking at Bob, the parrot that she had inherited when her parents died. "It isn't necessary that it be pleasurable. Only that it be successful." And that it actually take place.

"Bob, I have got to be enticing," she declared.

Bob tilted his head and didn't say a word. Well, eventually he did say "hellfire," which was Bob's favorite word, probably because it got him a lot of attention from strangers. Maybe also because it had been her father's favorite word, and Bob had been with Dennis Holbrook for years.

"*Hellfire* is just the word, though," she said, looking in her mirror and seeing what she always saw, a drab woman who faded into the woodwork. Under ordinary circumstances she liked fading. She chose to fade.

For a second she was tempted to rush to the phone, call Caleb and tell him that everything had been a mistake. But she refused to back down. She didn't want to wake up one more day feeling unfulfilled.

"So we improvise," she said, digging through her closet and pulling out one of her mother's strapless red dresses, a little number that Barbara Holbrook had been especially fond of. It was probably a little too tight, but she would just have to deal with that.

Next, Victoria sat down to struggle with the unfamiliar pile of makeup that was spread out in front of her. She had driven to the next town to buy it, afraid that someone would see her and wonder if she had gone completely mad. Victoria Holbrook never wore makeup.

Forty-five minutes later she got up from the makeup table, not completely sure if she had got it right.

"Hellfire!" Bob said.

"I hope that means that I look okay and not like something out of a horror movie," Victoria muttered.

She picked up the dress and proceeded to shimmy into it. "Uh-oh," she said.

"Uh-oh, uh-oh," Bob mimicked.

"This won't do at all. There's too much me and not nearly enough dress," Victoria moaned. "I can't let Caleb see me like this. I wanted him to see me as a woman he would consider sleeping with once or twice. I did not want to look like a woman who gets drunk and dances on tabletops."

Frantically she slid hangers back and forth in the closet. Black suits. Black-and-white suits. Gray suits. More black suits.

And then the doorbell was ringing. Caleb was already here.

Victoria gave Bob a distressed look. "Don't even say it," she ordered.

But it was too late. "Hellfire," Bob squawked, saying exactly what Victoria was thinking.

Her dreams were about to go up in a blaze of strapless red satin.

She only hoped that Caleb Fremont was not the kind of man to talk. If he was, then her reputation was probably going the way of her dreams.

But, of course he was the kind of man to talk. He was a newspaper reporter.

"Hellfire," she said, and she stomped to the door and threw it open. Somehow she just couldn't manage a smile. This night was going to be a total disaster. She might as well send the man home right now.

But she wouldn't. She knew that she wouldn't. As Bob was her witness, she was going to wade in and do her best to see this thing through.

Caleb stared down at the vision before him and barely managed to keep from gulping. He was a man who prided himself on knowing a lot about women, but standing here looking down at Victoria Holbrook's full red lips, her creamy shoulders and her heaving… Well, there was a whole lot more of Victoria exposed than he had ever expected to experience.

She was frowning. Somewhere in the background someone was chanting the word *hellfire*. What's more, Victoria was clad in red. Not black. Not white. Not gray. Sexy, sassy, hot red. For a moment, Caleb wondered if he hadn't wandered into the wrong house. Maybe Victoria had a twin sister.

"I could come back another time if you like," he said. "If this is a bad time."

"Why would you say that?" She lifted her chin, a defiant gesture, even though she appeared to be trembling. Interesting. He wondered how many people had ever seen this woman defiant.

Delicious. Intriguing.

Caleb couldn't help chuckling. She was…well, she was rather pretty when she was miffed. There was a spark about her. He wondered what she would do if he told her that she looked explosively pretty. Would she slap his face? Crawl back into her shell?

"Mr. Fremont?" She sounded worried. Couldn't have that.

"Forgive me, Victoria. It's just that you look as if…"

She hastily glanced down at her cleavage, as if she had followed his own line of sight to the pretty shadow between her breasts. He almost thought he heard her moan. She was obviously not happy.

He squelched his smile and reached out, tipping her chin up away from that glorious view with his thumb. "Do you want to tell me what's going on, Victoria?

And…why exactly are you frowning at me in that very dissatisfied way? You did invite me here."

She made a visible attempt to smooth away her frown and failed. She lifted her face higher, as if to lift her chin from his touch. As she did, he felt her swallow beneath his fingertips. His head swam a bit, and he forced himself to remember that she was a neighbor, a colleague, and that she was a very private person who probably didn't like the fact that he was touching her. He shoved his hand in his pocket.

"*Did* I come at a bad time?" he asked, trying to figure out what was going on here.

She clasped her hands tightly in front of her. "No, I'm sorry. This is the right time. I was just…oh, I wasn't really frowning at *you*."

He looked behind him as if he expected there to be another man standing there. The one she had worn the red dress for.

"I'm not the only one then? You're expecting someone else?"

She shook her head and her chin-length sable hair swished against her cheeks. "No, no, come in. It's just us. I'm really all right. I just lost track of time and was caught off guard when the bell rang."

And she stepped back, as if to let him inside.

The heel of her lacy shoe caught on the carpeting, and he stepped forward, reaching out to keep her from stumbling. As he grasped her arms, she took a deep breath, her breasts shoving up against the red satin in a dangerous fashion.

Caleb did his best to ignore the enticing sight. He released her as soon as she was steady, and with his right hand, he reached back and shut the door behind him.

"Are you sure you're feeling all right, Victoria?" he couldn't help asking. He frowned and gave in to the urge to study her more fully. He stared openly.

She took a deep and visible breath and gave him an anxious look.

"Am I—do I have something wrong with my face?" she asked suddenly. "I wouldn't be at all surprised if I did." She gave a small laugh, an attempt to appear nonchalant. Didn't fool him a bit. This lady was way out of her element.

And then, he couldn't seem to stop himself, especially after she had just given him an excuse to do what he was dying to do. He touched her again, sliding his hand beneath her jaw this time. Carefully he turned her head this way and that. She had applied the whole shot: eye makeup, lipstick, powder. He loved the scent of powder. It smelled like...woman.

Alarms were going off inside him. Something in Caleb told him that he ought to be walking out right now. Under any other circumstances he would have been. If she had been any other woman, he would have been positive that this dinner, this dress, the makeup, the whole situation reeked of seduction.

He was fine with seduction. In fact, he was better than fine with seduction in the right place and time. This wasn't either of those, and for a man with his past and his habits, it would be the height of stupidity to mix business or community and pleasure. He had always known that, and so he should have been making his excuses and leaving, saying something tactful and friendly as he carefully extricated himself from the situation.

But something didn't fit here at all. This was Victoria Holbrook. And she didn't dress like this, she didn't ever look like this, and he would swear on everything he held dear in life she didn't practice seduction, or even want to.

Did she?

Chapter Three

Victoria gazed up at Caleb and wondered what in the world had ever given her the idea she could go through with this.

He was looking at her as if he was working on a jigsaw puzzle and had lost the very last piece. Men didn't look wary or confused when they were in the throes of passion.

"Caleb?"

"You're fine, Victoria," he told her. "Very fine. Nothing out of place at all. You look extremely…"

His voice was low. He stared at her, and for a minute his eyes looked fierce. He leaned closer. She had trouble breathing and felt as if all her internal organs were playing musical chairs inside her.

"I look…what?" she asked, nearly choking. It was so difficult to talk when he was this near. Of course, it had been years since she had been this close to a man, but she didn't quite remember it being like this. No doubt she had forgotten.

"You look absolutely… You look positively…"

He scrubbed one hand back through his hair, a sudden flash of exasperation in his eyes, and suddenly Victoria couldn't take it any longer. What had she been thinking? She wasn't some femme fatale and never had been. Hadn't she learned that a long time ago? Hadn't any attempt she'd ever made to stand out from the crowd, to shine, to draw attention to herself met with an embarrassing episode? Not that she was pitying herself. She was many fine things. She was a good businesswoman, loyal and true and honest. And also she was smart, very smart, so why, oh why was she making herself look so stupid right now?

She glanced up into Caleb's eyes. His expression was dark and unreadable. He looked amazingly handsome and not at all happy.

Victoria blew out a breath. "This was a mistake, a very bad idea," she said out loud, although it was really herself she was talking to.

Caleb lifted a brow. Her temperature rose slightly. Well, why not? The man was just devastatingly masculine.

"What was?" he asked.

"This." She lifted the skirt of the red dress and held it out. She lifted her face and pointed to her eyes and her lips.

"It doesn't look like a mistake," he said in that deep voice that rumbled through her, sinking into her skin and her bones and her soul.

"Good," she said suddenly with a small laugh. "But it was."

He frowned again. "Victoria, tell me something."

She looked up into those silver-blue eyes and waited.

"Did you or did you not tell me just this afternoon that you had no interest in me?"

Well, yes, she had said that, even though her erratic breathing told her that she had been a liar. He was handsome and masculine and virile and intelligent. Of course she was interested. All women would be. But with her it was different.

"I said that, yes," she said, her voice weak. "I meant it. And then—darn it, Caleb, I can't go through with this. This is all wrong. Let's start over. You go outside, I'll change clothes and wash my face and then you come back in, and we'll do this right."

He smiled then. Oh dear, she was amusing him. He wasn't taking her seriously. What a depressing thought.

"How about we just sit down right here and now, and you tell me what it is you want from me," he suggested softly.

"You won't like it," she confided. "I knew you wouldn't. I thought I might try to look and act like some of the women you date, catch you off guard, convince you."

"Convince me to do what?" he asked.

"But I'm clearly no good with this seduction business. I knew that, of course. The fact that I even thought of trying is just one more example of how desperate I've become."

"You're desperate?" he asked gently, and somehow

he was taking her by the arms and walking her backward slowly, easing her onto a couch. He sat beside her and she nearly jumped out of her skin. "Victoria," he said, "tell me what's wrong."

And then she couldn't help it. Looking into his eyes, she couldn't seem to think clearly, to choose her words wisely. Besides, she had never been any good at playing. Blunt and truthful had always been her way.

"I want you to give me a baby."

He sucked in his breath, and she knew she had done this all wrong. "A business deal, of course," she told him, leaning closer to him, his jacket brushing the naked skin of her arm. She bit her lips and tried to backpedal. "That is, I never really meant to trick you into something. The dress was an extremely bad idea. So was the makeup. I just thought it might make it easier for you to envision us…doing business. I'm really not asking all that much of you. I'm pretty sure it wouldn't take that much time and I wouldn't want more than just the basics. Actually, all you really have to do is…that is, all I need for you to do is…"

"Don't," Caleb said, holding up one hand. His voice sounded strained. "I think I have a pretty good idea of what you and I would be doing together."

She was pretty sure he did, too. She was also sure that he was going to turn her down.

"I've offended you, haven't I? And instead of looking convincing, I merely look ridiculous, and you're uncomfortable. Please accept my apologies," she said, looking down at her hands, and she couldn't help the sadness that entered her voice, even though she hated having people feel sorry for her.

"Victoria," Caleb said. He ducked his head to look into her eyes. "I don't even know you, but I do know that this isn't you. Does this baby mean so much to you, then?"

She refused to look at him. He had seen her at her most vulnerable, her most awkward and ridiculous. She had done the kind of thing she'd been running from all her life, exposing herself. And it had all been for nothing.

"Victoria," he said, more gently, and she was very afraid he was going to move even closer, that he would see too deep inside her soul.

She raised her head and forced herself to take a deep breath, to push her emotions aside, to try to speak firmly. "There are so many things I want to share and experience. To hold a baby close, to sing him to sleep, to make sure that nothing bad happens to him, to…just to love him and let him know that he's special. I—it sounds silly, maybe maudlin, certainly a cliché, but I've always wanted a child."

"I respect that, but there are other ways."

"I'm aware. I've looked at the options, but I don't trust sperm banks. How do you really know that the donor isn't just some guy hard up on his luck, someone who would steal an old lady's handbag except for the fact that donating sperm for cash is easier and more enjoyable?"

She looked directly at Caleb, and to her relief he wasn't laughing. Well, he was almost smiling, the right corner of his lips lifting in that way he had, but he wasn't laughing.

"Adoption?" he suggested.

"Maybe," she agreed, "but if I can, just once I want

to experience the whole thing, beginning to end, including labor. It's important to me. Otherwise, I would never have done this. Never."

"I think I know that," he said. "This isn't like you, is it?" He fingered the slick material of her dress.

Unfortunately, no, it wasn't. At all.

"I really don't do froufrou very well," she said. "I'm a woman of very basic tastes. I like black."

"And white," he added. "I'm sure I've seen you in black and white."

"Yes."

"No makeup or at least not much."

"No, not in years. Makeup is gooey, uncomfortable and I'm a bit allergic to parts of it." She blinked her eyes, which were beginning to sting.

"Must have wanted this pretty badly to put on a froufrou red dress and makeup that stings."

"I do. Time is running out for me."

"You said you were thirty-six. That isn't ancient by any means."

"My eggs are getting older every day. Maybe they don't work right anymore."

"Unlikely."

"But possible. They're virgins."

She thought she heard Caleb suck in a breath. He rose and looked down at her.

"Victoria, you understand that it *has* been an honor to be asked to be the father of your child. I guess I'm a little shocked and more than a little flattered. No one in town would ever consider me father material."

"You wouldn't actually have to be a father," she said

quickly, seeing her opportunity slip away. It was obvious that the next word out of his mouth was going to be *but.* He was honored, *but…*

"I understood what you meant," he said, "and I truly hope you find a solution. I would reconsider the sperm-bank option if I were you. But I'm afraid I'm the wrong man for the job."

She wanted to tell him that he wasn't, but obviously he *was* the wrong man. Because he didn't want the job.

She nodded. "I appreciate your time," she said, managing a smile as she rose. Now that everything had fallen apart, she felt exposed and raw. She reached down and grabbed an afghan and started to unfold it.

Caleb reached out and took it from her. He finished what she had started, then draped the cream-colored afghan about her shoulders. He stroked the knuckle of one finger across her lips.

"You are a very gutsy lady, Victoria. I really hope that you make your dreams come true."

She shrugged. "Don't worry. I will," she said, and then she showed Caleb out the door.

Caleb felt as if there was a car race taking place inside his brain. What was going on here?

Little, quiet, unprepossessing Victoria Holbrook, who rarely smiled, who was all but invisible to the citizens of Renewal and kept mostly to her bookstore and her books, had just sprouted butterfly wings and an undeniably shapely body and had made a pass at him?

"No, not a pass, you dolt. It's not you she's interested in. Just your genetic material." Which was, he had to admit, the first time a woman had been interested in that particular part of him. Women had occasionally wanted him for fun, love, marriage, commitment of any kind he was willing to give, a positive story in the newspaper and often just for sex, but not one had ever coveted only his DNA.

She had implied that she was no good at seduction.

"Well, she's sure as heck wrong," he muttered, shoving open the door of the newspaper office the next morning.

"Who's wrong?" Denise asked.

"You are."

She frowned. "About what?"

"About the fact that I have no integrity where women are concerned." Not that he was about to explain himself and give away Victoria's secret.

"Hmm," Denise said. "Does that mean you've decided to become celibate?"

Caleb almost cringed. He thought of Victoria in her pretty red dress with her luminous sad brown eyes telling him that she wanted him to give her a baby and then being such a good sport when he told her that he couldn't do that. He thought of how her bare skin had felt when he'd brushed against her. Celibate?

"Maybe," he agreed. Because he sure wasn't going to lay hands on Victoria. Touching her could only lead to more, which would lead to him acting like a jerk somewhere down the road. He'd seen too much of that when his father had broken his mother's heart and then broken it again and yet again until she had become a scared and lonely and disheartened shell of the woman she had once been. And Caleb had also seen it in the eyes of good, kind women who had just had the misfortune to think he was something better and more decent than he was, women whose hearts he had unintentionally broken and whose pride he had damaged without meaning to. He'd seen it in reverse when his vibrant best friend's wife had dumped him, leaving a ghost of a man behind. There were no winners in such situations. Better, far better to steer clear of the situations. That way no one got hurt and no one ended up feeling like the scum of the earth for not being able to reciprocate another's emotions.

So how could he take Victoria up on her offer? He'd seen how vulnerable she was, and there was no way he would risk adding to her misery. There would be absolutely *no* touching her again. In any manner.

"You? Caleb Fremont? Celibate?" Denise was saying, rolling her eyes. "I'll believe that when pigs put on pink tutus and do the dance of the sugarplum fairies."

Victoria had shapely dancer's legs beneath that red dress, Caleb couldn't help remembering. With knees a man could worship with his mouth. He'd caught just a glimpse when she'd sat down. A most tantalizing glimpse, and the thought of Victoria Holbrook showing him her legs by choice rather than chance suddenly made everything that made him male shift into overdrive.

"Caleb? You didn't answer me. What act of integrity did you perform today?" his assistant asked.

He growled at Denise. "I walked away from a beautiful woman offering herself to me."

Denise raised her brows. "You? Why?"

Caleb dropped into his chair and began to shuffle papers. "Because she deserved better. Now can we—"

"I know. Can we get this paper out? You want to work after making a statement like that?"

Yes, he did. In fact, work was all he wanted to concentrate on. When he covered the news, everything was clear, truthful, honest and honorable. There were only the facts, no disturbing choices, no temptations, no dangerous emotions that could ruin lives. Just cold, clear, hard facts.

Man, he loved this newspaper. It had been his salvation after that ugly business with his fiancée, Marie. Even now he could taste the guilt.

He needed this newspaper, and he was not going to change his line of work and go into the business of supplying his chromosomes to women who wanted to give pregnancy a whirl. He was never in this lifetime going to let his fingers roam over Victoria Holbrook.

Not even over one of her pretty little knees.

He didn't even get near any woman who didn't understand that he was just for fun, a roller coaster with no purpose, just a few quick thrills and some laughs before heading home to the serious business of work. He had rules, and on those occasional instances when he dated, he firmly enforced them. And now he had a completely new rule.

Caleb Fremont was not making love for the purpose of impregnating a woman.

No matter how nicely she asked.

Heavens, he didn't really even know Victoria Holbrook. And if she wanted him to father her child, she knew even less about him.

"He was perfect, Bob. Just what I wanted," Victoria said two days later. "Look, I did an extensive search on the man, using his own newspaper and whatever resources I could find on the Internet. I asked discreet questions of customers about what they thought of the Renewal *Gazette* and its editor-in-chief. Not one person said a bad thing about him. Many complimented him on his intelligence, his integrity, his dignity, his fairness and his commitment to doing a good job and telling the truth. You saw how kind and gentle he was with me, never once telling me that I was acting crazy when you and I both know that I was. It was completely out of character, my stepping into the limelight like that, trying to get his attention. Mom and Dad would have been proud."

"Dad," Bob said, and Victoria could have sworn there was a sad, wistful tone in the old parrot's voice.

"Yes, well, I miss him, too, the old show-off." Her parents had been born performers. It had almost broken their hearts that she was so different, so petrified of the limelight. But they had still loved her. It had not been a hardship to take care of them the last few years of their lives until they had died within days of each other just over two years ago. That was when she had come to Renewal, because she needed a fresh start and the town was the right size. Relatively small and comfortable, Renewal hadn't had a single bookstore. There had been a place for her, a niche to call her own. She had liked the look of the town immediately with its old-fashioned houses, its massive oaks and its wide, quiet streets, some of them still redbrick. And, yes, she had liked the name, even though she knew it was silly to move to a town because it had a name that promised that a person could begin again.

She had done all right these past two years. Her business wasn't thriving, but it gave her a comfortable living, people respected her privacy and didn't demand more of her than she felt she could give, and the slow, easy pace the town moved at suited her. If only she weren't so lonely. If only she had her child. Bob was great, but he was old and he wasn't human, even if he seemed to think he was.

"I'll have to try some other route, Bob. We want to do this well and right. I don't want to invite just any man into my bed." In fact, when Victoria looked at most of the men in the town, she couldn't even begin to imagine being naked with one of them. Her stomach protested at the thought. But that was probably just some defect in her, because she was sure that there must be other good men in the town. It was silly to be so cowardly.

"Caleb would have been perfect." She remembered the gentle way he had wrapped the afghan around her, the way her heart had thudded strong and loud when he had looked at her. She would not have been afraid to let Caleb touch her.

But Caleb didn't want to give her a baby. She couldn't force him to want her or to do her bidding.

All she could do was try some alternate route.

* * *

The copy came across his desk three days after his evening with Victoria. Caleb wasn't sure how many other desks it had crossed before it came to his, and he only saw it because Denise was out with a cold, and he had taken over her task of proofing the paper before it went to print.

It was a simple blind ad.

Wanted: a virile man of intelligence and good character to father a child. Will pay one thousand dollars up front and four thousand more once conception takes place. No future commitments once the goal is accomplished. Must supply five character references and three business references. Send responses to Future Mom, P.O. Box B482 in Dalloway, Illinois. No married men need apply.

"Hell. Double hell." Caleb all but shouted the words.

"Something wrong, Caleb?" Stan Ritchie peered around the corner of the next room.

Only that he felt as if the top of his head was about to detonate, Caleb thought.

"I'll be back in ten. Or maybe twenty," he said, sparing Stan the briefest glance before grabbing up the piece of paper and heading out the door onto the street.

In the two blocks between the *Gazette* and the bookstore, Caleb nearly ran over two elderly men and a lady walking her dog, he was moving so fast and with such intent. Muttering swift apologies and making sure everyone was okay and still standing, Caleb moved on.

He pushed open the door to the bookstore with a bit more force than was necessary.

The normally quiet and somewhat dark little bookstore was a buzz of people and light. Caleb stopped dead in his tracks. He had forgotten. Victoria was changing her image, and now she had clouds and stars and fiction and children's books and couches. Flowers. Cookies. Punch. And obviously a whole store full of women.

Everyone looked up as the door hit the wall and the bell clattered out of control.

He located her among the crowd in a split second. His eyes felt like red lasers.

She blinked those pretty brown eyes of hers wide.

"Mr. Fremont?" she asked.

Mister Fremont? *Mister* Fremont, when only three days ago she had been asking him to take her to bed and plant his seed inside her?

And today she was advertising for some other man to do the same.

"We have to talk," he said, ignoring the other people in the room.

She looked around at the amassed crowds. "I don't think we can do that. I can't just leave. I have customers."

He pulled out the ever-present notepad and pen that he kept tucked in his back pocket. "For IOUs, in case someone finds a book they want," he said, stepping into the store and placing the notepad next to her register. "For the sin of interrupting your shopping, I'll pay for the first book that anyone buys in the next hour," he said to the crowd, but he didn't take his eyes off Victoria.

There was a worried and confused look in her eyes. "That's hardly necessary."

"My asking you to come with me might be costing you business, and that's what you and I are all about, isn't it? Business?"

His voice dropped low, as he meant it to. Her chin came up, defiant.

"I never implied otherwise."

Exactly. She was thinking of making a baby, damn it all, and she considered it purely business. Now she was soliciting men in the newspaper. Caleb couldn't help wondering if she had approached other men before coming to him. Didn't the woman know that there were plenty of men who would take advantage of her? Men who had no interest in her baby project but plenty of interest simply in sliding sneakily into her bed?

He could tell, looking into her wide eyes, that she didn't have a clue. What had she told him? That she had virgin genes? His anger and his temperature rose.

"Come on," he said, holding out his hand. She eyed it as if he had just offered her a crocodile to cuddle.

All eyes were on them now. The two of them were the center of attention. She looked around, and he could almost swear she jerked. She put her hands behind her back and twisted them nervously.

"If you're that worried about the bookstore," he said, his voice a bit more gentle, "then I'll make it worth your while. Place an order for fifty copies of whatever yesterday's bestseller was." He knew that much about her store from an article the paper had run on local businesses. Every day she had a blackboard that listed the previous day's bestseller.

Victoria arched a brow. "Are you absolutely sure about that? The distributor delivered fiction and these other things bright and early this morning, but yesterday I was still dealing only in historical volumes."

"Doesn't matter."

"You're sure?" Her voice sounded unnaturally high. A customer cleared her throat. What was this all about?

"All right, tell me," he said. "What *was* yesterday's bestseller?"

Some woman twittered. Ginnie Ashland. "Something that's right up your alley, Caleb," she said, picking up the small chalkboard and holding it so that it faced him. Yesterday's bestseller was listed as being *The History and Trivia of Contraception.*

Victoria had the decency to look uncomfortable. Not that Ginnie's opinion was in any way Victoria's fault. He was pretty sure no one knew what she had proposed to him. He was the one who had allowed people to think he was an insatiable skirt-chaser, and he was the one, therefore, who had invited the laughter. That didn't bother him at all, but he could see the guilt in Victoria's eyes.

"I'll come with you," Victoria suddenly said. "Forget the books."

"I'll take the offer of your company," he said, "but we're not forgetting the books. I don't go back on my promises. Fifty copies," he reiterated.

And he took her hand and pulled her from the store. Her soft skin slid pleasantly beneath his fingers. He couldn't help picturing Victoria thumbing through a book on contraception and then tossing that book aside, because when *she* made love to a man, there would be nothing between his skin and hers except air.

Somehow he managed to keep breathing. He tugged harder, which brought her closer to him. A mistake, he realized as his temperature began to spiral higher.

Once outside the store, Victoria pulled up short. She faced him, deliberately staring him down.

"Caleb, what on earth are you so upset about?" she asked. "I didn't want to ask with so many people about, but now we're more or less alone, and I think I deserve to know what has made you so angry. I could understand if you were mad at me the other day, but I apologized for that. I thought you and I were done."

So had he.

He brandished the copy for the ad. "Did you write this?"

She read it carefully, calmly. "I believe I did. What of it?"

He leaned closer, his body almost touching hers. By all that was newsworthy, she was driving him insane with that matter-of-fact attitude, those clear brown eyes and that compact little body of hers. That body she was going to give to the first good man—or bad man—to say yes to her demands.

"You, Ms. Holbrook," he said, purposely using the name he knew she hated, "have a lot to learn about men."

She looked up at him. She studied him and bit that lower lip again. It was all he could do to keep himself from reaching out, pulling her close and having his own taste of her pretty mouth. "Are you going to teach me?" she suddenly and quietly asked.

Caleb took a deep breath. "Definitely. Let's go to your place and I'll tell you what you need to know."

And then he couldn't help himself. He leaned closer, swooped in and kissed her once, hard.

She gasped beneath his mouth, which made him crazy, but he managed to raise his head and release her.

"What was that?" she asked, her voice coming out a bit shaky.

"That," he said, "was the first lesson."

Which made absolutely no sense at all, but Caleb didn't care. The need to kiss Victoria had gone beyond reason. Now that he knew that her lips did feel as good as they looked, he could stop wondering. They could both, he hoped, move on and somehow solve her problem in a way that wouldn't make him completely insane.

Chapter Four

Victoria's brain was just not working properly. She couldn't seem to manage one rational thought. But her lips…her lips were tingling, burning. She longed to touch them, but then Caleb would know that he was right. There were lots of things she didn't know about men and one of those was how this man whom she barely even knew could make her ache like this.

"Why are you so angry?" she said, finally stopping at the end of her street and digging her heels in.

Caleb's hand tightened on her own and he turned to face her.

"You don't want to discuss this in the middle of the street, do you?" he asked, a frown creasing his brows.

His silver-blue eyes stared into hers and for a moment she didn't know what she wanted. Then Victoria glanced over her shoulder. There weren't many people around, but there was Caleb, and Caleb was looking at her as if he could see right through the slate-gray suit she was wearing. Suddenly Victoria felt naked. Worse, she suddenly felt as if she wanted to be naked, which was pretty much a momentous and first-time thing for her, at least where a man was concerned. How humiliating if anyone should guess, especially if that anyone should be Caleb, who had already told her that he didn't want to sleep with her. Did she really want anyone else to witness whatever humiliating words should pass between them today?

Victoria squared her shoulders, raised her chin and gave Caleb what she hoped was a haughty glance. "All right, I'll humor you, Mr. Fremont," she said, carefully stepping around him and leading him to her door.

For a minute, she thought she heard a choked sound behind her, but it was followed quickly by what could only be a chuckle. Caleb Fremont was laughing at her!

Victoria wanted to run. Caleb had turned her down, he'd seen her at her most awkward, he had made her do stupid things like wearing a red dress she had no business wearing, he had witnessed Bob's embarrassing parrot cursing. Then he'd kissed her and made her lips burn even though the kiss had obviously meant nothing to him, and now? Now he was laughing at her. She had never felt more self-conscious walking into her house than she did this minute. Caleb's eyes were on her, probably measuring her up, comparing her to other women he'd known. Womanly women who knew how to wear a slinky red dress and makeup. Women who knew how to make a man salivate at the thought of sleeping with them. Not women like her. Well, that was all right. After all, in spite of her earlier decision that he would be the perfect sperm donor, Caleb Fremont was really nothing to her. She didn't really know him and now she never would. She had made a mistake when she had chosen him, but now she could move on.

Victoria could barely wait to move on and put Caleb and his kiss out of her mind. She whirled as soon as he had closed the door behind him.

"Mr. Fremont," she began, not waiting for him to start lecturing her. "This is hardly necessary. I assure you that I'm old enough to do as I please. I'm a grown woman."

He slowly shook his head. "Sorry, but you're not even close."

She sucked in her breath, wounded in spite of herself. "I'm older than you," she said, the words coming out wispier than she would have wished. "I'm thirty-six. You're only thirty-four." Saying the words out loud was somehow humbling and humiliating. She had thrown herself at a younger man and he had rejected her. Not that it mattered or that she really cared. This wasn't about caring, after all, was it? It was about simple procreation. Science. Business.

Caleb still hadn't spoken.

Victoria crossed her arms in a protective gesture and tried to look haughty and superior and older than she felt.

A small amused look twinkled in Caleb's eyes and then faded fast. She supposed she had sounded rather childish. Maybe she even looked foolish.

"Two years is nothing, Victoria, but I'm not talking years," he said, leaning close, "and I'm not talking about how you look, either, because believe me, you look as if you're completely, officially and very voluptuously grown up, which is a very real part of the problem." His voice dropped a bit, and she bit her lip. She tried not to think about how much experience Caleb had in assessing women's bodies.

"All right then, you're not talking physically mature. I have a master's degree," she said, "if you're insulting my intelligence."

"I'm not," he assured her. "I have no doubt that you're a very intelligent lady, but that doesn't mean a thing, given the course you've chosen to follow."

"I thought that ad over very carefully."

"You invited a group of total strangers to come sample your body." He held out the copy so that she could read it.

She refused to look. "I know what it says. I wrote it. Remember?"

"Ah, yes, you did," he said, staring directly into her eyes as if trying to read her mind. "I wonder what you were thinking when you typed this out."

"I was thinking that I wanted a baby, of course, and that there are other ways than the usual of acquiring them."

"We've already discussed some of those ways. You've dismissed them. I believe you're still planning on conceiving this baby the old-fashioned way, skin to skin."

His voice was a low suggestive whisper. Victoria struggled to breathe.

"Of course," she managed.

"Of course. And what did you think your…prospective audience would think when they read this?" he asked, looking down at the paper he still held.

She knew what he was implying. "I did my best to make it sound like a business deal. That's what I intend it to be."

He shook his head slowly. "Men don't think that way."

"They don't make business deals? Of course they do."

"Oh, yes, they make deals, but it's never strictly business when a man slips inside a woman's body."

Somehow she managed to keep breathing. She struggled to speak, but he was there before her.

"Victoria, this could be dangerous. It *is* dangerous. Don't do it."

"I've insisted on references."

"People can fake references. They can buy them. You've given them plenty of incentive."

"It's not that much money."

"It's money and sex and no strings attached. There are plenty of men who would consider that winning the lottery. Unscrupulous men. You *can't* do this."

But Victoria had had enough. "You can't know what I'm feeling or thinking. You can't be in my head and my life and know what I need and want and how much I need and want a baby. I've made up my mind. I want my baby, and so, yes, I'm going to do this, Caleb, and I won't be lectured like a child. I've been on my own for two years now, longer if you consider the fact that my parents had been ill for a long time before that. I've proven that I can run my own life. So you needn't be concerned, because I don't intend to do anything stupid. I'm not going to let just any man into my bed."

Caleb looked to one side and blew out his breath.

"You asked me into your bed, Victoria. Most people would say that that wasn't very smart."

"Then they would be wrong. I researched you thoroughly before I asked." But she had been wrong. Very wrong. He had been opposed to her proposition. Caleb certainly hadn't felt that the prospect of having sex with her was comparable to winning the lottery. Not by a long shot.

"There are some aspects of a man you can't unearth with simple written research." His voice and words implied that some of those aspects might involve physical contact. Victoria swallowed hard.

"I don't need to know everything. Just the types of things that involve my safety and my baby's genetics."

"I'm not sure that's good enough."

"It will have to be good enough." Victoria looked up into his eyes and thought she saw concern. For her safety. Of course, he was concerned. He was a good guy. It showed in his writing. That was part of the reason she had chosen him, because no matter how promiscuous he might be, he had absolutely no record of harming women. He had rallied to their causes in his work. Women gravitated to him. They desired him. They loved him. Part of that had to be because he treated them with this kind of gallantry.

Immediately Victoria felt her grumpy mood soften slightly. Caleb hadn't asked to be involved in her life; she had dragged him in. She had made him feel responsible. Now she had to let him off the hook. And so she gave Caleb a small smile. She felt a moment of deep regret that he would not be the one to father her child. She tried not to think about the fact that that meant she would never get to experience the kind of intimacy that other women experienced with him. That couldn't matter, not to a woman like herself. She wouldn't let it.

She ignored the overly fast beating of her heart and stepped closer to him. "I appreciate your concern, Caleb, but you don't have to do this. I'm sure everything will be fine, and I promise you that I'll be careful. I'll— I'll Google any promising candidates, and I won't take the final step until I'm absolutely comfortable."

"And when will you feel comfortable?" Caleb asked, suddenly placing one hand on the wall behind her head and leaning closer to her. Victoria swallowed hard. Her self-assured act disappeared just like that, and her heart began to racket out of control. She had rarely been aware of herself as a woman. Not a surprise, since she wasn't the physical type. Or at least she hadn't been before. Now, it was as if all the years of not feeling feminine had culminated in one big backlog of feminine awareness and pent-up desire. Too bad it was happening with a man who had absolutely no interest in her.

"When?" he repeated.

She pressed her palms back against the wall. She tried to make her breathing even and failed. "Um…when I know it's safe," she managed to whisper.

Caleb groaned. "That's impossible. Victoria, you're offering men money to make love with you. A man who would sign on for that probably doesn't have any scruples."

"I don't need scruples. Just someone healthy and intelligent and clean. You understand that, Caleb? I want the best that I can get, but I'm not really looking for much."

"Well, you should definitely ask for more," Caleb said. He pushed away from the wall.

She didn't answer. Obviously he didn't understand.

"I can't talk you out of this?" he asked.

She bit down on her lip. "You could," she somehow managed to say, "but you said you couldn't be the one."

A pained look crossed his face. She was instantly sorry that she had reminded him of her former request. It was humiliating and it obviously made him feel bad.

"It's not in me to do that, Victoria," he said. "Not even if you're not looking for much."

She nodded. "All right, then. It's no problem. But I will do it my way. You have to accept that. It's really not your concern, anyway. I never meant to involve you this much. It was supposed to be very simple and short and done. I apologize for tangling you up in all of this, but you can stop now. I'm capable. I'm fine."

Caleb blew out a breath. He didn't say okay. He didn't say anything. He simply walked toward the door. When he reached it and opened it, he stood in the opening, then turned back toward her. "I could nix this ad," he said.

She stared at him. "There are other towns and papers."

"I noticed that you took the   in Dalloway. Why?"

"I didn't want everyone to know how desperate I was. I didn't want anyone to know what was going on until it was a done deal."

But she had asked him. She knew that had to be going through his head. It was certainly going through hers.

"You were a mistake, I guess," she said hesitantly. "I shouldn't have involved you."

"But you did," he said, "and there's no changing that." And then he was out the door.

She wondered what he meant by that.

All right, he had let her run the damn ad, just as she had written it. It was her right, after all, and he really had no business interfering. But a week had passed and Caleb couldn't help wondering just what was going on. Had she received any answers to her ad? Of course she had. What kind of men had responded? And what kind of mail was she receiving?

The possibilities made him blanch. Men being what they were, he could only imagine the kind of slime some men were sending to her post office box, or the lies that they were trying to pass off on her.

It galled him that she felt she had to offer money for some guy to have the night of his life.

It galled him even more that he was completely out of the loop. She had come to him for help and he had been of no help at all. It wasn't the first time he had been unable to help a woman in need, but hadn't he learned even one thing about being useful over the years? And why was he just sitting here when heaven knows what was happening on the baby-making front?

He got up from his desk and headed for the door.

"Where are you off to?" Denise's voice was loud and somewhat shrill. "It's not lunchtime yet, and didn't you just tell me that we needed to get the next edition ready yesterday?"

He didn't turn. Denise was right. "Something came up. It won't take long," he said and then he strode out the door, ignoring the dagger-sharp stares Denise was no doubt stabbing into his back. He knew that his too-curious assistant would watch him all the way down the street and that she would talk later. For Victoria's sake he regretted that, but it couldn't be helped.

Caleb made a beeline for Victoria's bookstore. He walked right past the twin planters she had recently placed outside the door, the ones filled with pink and white New Guinea impatiens, the ones that signaled the world that she was making a change in her life. She was nesting, he realized. Making her world soft for her baby.

The thought made him weak.

He couldn't afford to be weak right now. Instead, he entered the store and saw that it was again filled with women, but he quickly located Victoria in the crowd. Amid this blue-and-white décor and the crowds of red-lipped women, she stood out in her crisp black and white like a single alabaster rose in a thicket of fiery poppies.

She was talking to little Allie McAllister, who was only four. Allie's family could barely make ends meet and some of the local merchants gave them discounts to help them get by. Most of those were for the basic necessities, but he had the feeling that Victoria would consider books a necessity, and even if she didn't, she could never turn away a child. Victoria's eyes were shining as the little girl said something to her in hushed and reverent tones.

"I like Sleeping Beauty's shoes, too," Victoria agreed,

"but they're not as pretty as yours, because yours have buckles. Very cool."

Allie giggled, her little face lighting up as she peered down at her hand-me-down shoes. She gave Victoria a smile and hugged the picture book she was holding before running over to sit on a bench next to her mother. She kicked her feet up and gazed at the buckles on her shoes.

Caleb turned his attention away from the child and noticed that the entire crowd had turned to stare at him. Probably because last time he had been in here, he had looked like a thundercloud and he had all but dragged Victoria from the store. In a town the size of Renewal such things were noted and remembered.

Well, that was just too bad. "Ladies," he said to the assembled crowd. "Pete," he said to the only male in their midst. And then he busied himself at the nearest stacks just as though he came into Victoria's bookstore all the time. He wanted to talk to her, but he had promised himself he wouldn't do what he'd done the last time and embarrass her by insisting on seeing her alone. Obviously he should have caught her on the way home from work. He wondered why he hadn't seemed to be able to wait.

Because you feel responsible for her being in this mess, he thought. And he didn't like her situation at all. He was pretty darn sure she wouldn't tell a soul if one of her prospective dads did something out of line. That was the way Victoria struck him. She thought she had to do everything on her own, including fighting for her honor and her personal safety.

As if he would let some guy get away with taking advantage of her.

But maybe someone had already tried and she hadn't said a thing. Maybe that was why she was looking so pale and nervous all of a sudden. He should wait until after work to see her.

Caleb glanced at his watch. He noticed that Allie and her mother had left. Some of the other customers had gone, too, including Pete. The remaining all-female crowd watched as he moved closer to Victoria.

Victoria was pressing her hands together in front of her. Nervously? No, why should he make her nervous? She had admitted that she wasn't interested in him.

"Care to have lunch with me, Victoria?" he asked, keeping his voice quiet and low.

She blinked and opened her mouth. She was going to tell him that she couldn't close the store.

He glanced at the book of the day. Damn. *How to Make a Man Beg to Please You* was written on the board in blue chalk. Oh, well.

"I'll take fifty copies," he said, nodding toward the board. "It will make a nice addition to the fifty new books I already have."

The women tittered. Some of them had been here the last time he'd tried to coax Victoria to come with him. She certainly was the most reluctant woman he'd met in a long time. Except for that day with the red dress.

Heat climbed up his body when he remembered how Victoria had looked with those creamy shoulders naked and those pretty knees exposed.

"You're sure ordering a lot of copies of single books, Caleb," one woman said. "You thinking of starting your own bookstore and giving Victoria some competition?"

What he was thinking of doing with Victoria didn't bear repeating right now, especially since he was never going to follow through. Especially since Victoria wasn't interested in him as a man other than as a sperm donor.

"I'm thinking that Victoria looks hungry," he said. "I'm feeling a little hungry myself. Fifty books," he told Victoria and held out his hand.

She stared at it as if he had offered her an indecent proposal when, in fact, he was sure that he hadn't voiced his thoughts of a moment ago.

Still she didn't take his hand. She didn't take one step closer to him.

"Make that one hundred copies," he said.

She blinked and opened her mouth. To protest, no doubt. His Victoria was certainly good at protesting.

"All right, one hundred fifty," he said softly, upping the ante.

"Must be losing your touch, Caleb," someone said. "I wonder how high she'll make you go. Thank goodness you're a wealthy man."

And that seemed to snap Victoria out of her stillness. "No copies," she said. "Actually, I was going to come ask *you* to lunch."

He raised his brows. She was practically shaking. She was the world's worst liar, and yet he had to hand it to her. Victoria Holbrook had guts. "I'll be back in half an hour," she told her customers.

She placed her hand in his, only a slight trembling revealing her discomfort. Then she moved toward the door with him.

"One hundred fifty copies," he insisted and looked

toward Julie Ashton, who he knew helped Victoria from time to time. "Go ahead and place the order, Julie. I'll pick them up when they come in. And don't expect her back for at least an hour. We're going to Dalloway."

Victoria glanced up at him quickly. For a minute he thought she was going to argue. He decided that he hoped she would. He was beginning to like arguing with Victoria. There was something very erotic about sparring with her, which probably meant he should refrain from doing so. Still, he waited for her to put him in his place.

Instead she looked up at him and smiled.

"That's a good choice, Caleb. I've been wanting to go to Dalloway all week."

Which meant she hadn't yet checked her post office box. Which meant this would be her very first batch of submissions. He should be happy that he could be there to help her sift through them.

Instead he merely felt grumpy. He couldn't think of one good reason why. Maybe it was because he had just ordered one hundred fifty copies of a book he would only end up donating to libraries across the country.

It was obvious that Victoria didn't need even one copy of *How To Make a Man Beg To Please You*. There were going to be plenty of men begging to please her very soon.

He wasn't one of them, but he wasn't happy about the others, either.

Chapter Five

It was a good thing that Dalloway was close, Victoria thought as they drove to the neighboring town. She was alone in a car with Caleb, too close to ignore how long his legs were or how he drove with such confidence. While his eyes were on the road, she couldn't help looking at him.

Unexpectedly he glanced her way and caught her staring. She squirmed on the seat.

"You're probably thinking that I have a lot of nerve," he said, not seeming to mind if that was what she thought. And it wasn't what she had been thinking at all. She had been thinking that he had a jaw that probably enticed women to place their lips there.

It was the most frivolous thought she could remember having had in years. And the most forbidden.

"You *do* have a lot of nerve." She tried to edge away

from her own thoughts. "I'm just wondering why. Why do you want to go with me to Dalloway? You think I'm going to find something there I can't deal with, don't you?"

He looked away from the road again for another half a second. "No, I think you'll deal with whatever you find and you'll be able to do it alone. But you shouldn't have to."

"You don't owe me anything just because I propositioned you."

And then he swore. She wasn't sure of what exactly he said because he said it beneath his breath, but it was definitely swearing.

"What?" she demanded.

"You don't beat around the bush, do you, Victoria? I hadn't thought of the invitation you issued to me as propositioning me."

She hadn't either. It sounded so cold, so crude, but...

"I don't believe in hiding from the truth. I asked you to sleep with me."

"No, asking a man to sleep with you in the sense you mean indicates a real desire to make love. That's not what you want. You just want the basics. No frills. No heat. Isn't that right?"

He glanced at her again, his eyes intense and inescapable. She wondered how many women had gazed into those eyes as Caleb had slid inside them.

She jumped.

"Victoria?"

"Just the basics," she agreed. "I don't want heat." Especially when it made her feel so uncomfortable and disgruntled. "And I don't expect anyone to help me."

"Obviously. You wouldn't have run that ad if you expected things of people. We wouldn't be driving out to peek in a post office box if you had expectations, but it's not a sin to want company, Victoria. This isn't the kind of thing you should have to go through alone."

He didn't understand. She had gone through everything in her life alone, or almost alone. Her parents had loved her, but they had been obsessed with each other and their work. She was so diffcrent from them that they had looked at her as some sort of sweet aberration, and they had left her mostly to her own devices. She was used to depending only on herself. It was dangerous to try and reach out. Reaching out got you stung.

"Victoria?"

She nodded. "Yes?"

"Let me do this."

"Out of responsibility?"

He hesitated. "I'm not sure what my motives are, but I am sure that I need to do this. At the very least, it's because we're neighbors and fellow businesspeople. Neighbors look out for each other's interests. How about that for a reason?"

That she understood. "All right, then," she said with a small smile. "I'll stop arguing."

Caleb laughed. It was a strong, clean and very masculine sound. Men had never laughed with her, she realized. "Good," he said, "because we're here." And he parked the car, went around it and drew her out. He placed one hand on the small of her back.

She jumped again. No man had touched her like that. It was a nothing touch, one that meant nothing, anyway.

She'd seen a thousand men do that with a thousand women. It was a casual touch, so why didn't it make her feel casual?

She tried to feign relaxation, but her body felt stiff. She was aware of every one of Caleb's fingers on her back.

Perhaps he didn't notice. She hoped he didn't. They walked up the steps of the post office.

"Box number B482?" he asked.

"You remembered." And she couldn't help grinning at that. But when she got to the small post office box and opened it, there was only a key and a note inside.

Caleb stiffened beside her. "Too much mail? They had to transfer everything to a larger box," he said, reading the note. And when Victoria had located the other box, her breathing almost stopped.

"Oh my. I hadn't expected…" She glanced up at Caleb, who was looking at her, not the huge stack of mail. His expression looked grim.

"Let's go eat. Then I'll take you back home. I think you're going to need some fuel and some time to sift through all this."

She couldn't think, she couldn't talk. Finally her brain began to function. "I have to return to the store. Julie…"

"Will understand that you're feeling the need to sit down now and then. She doesn't have to know why. You're the owner."

She hesitated, then nodded. "All right. You're right. I do need some time to drink all this in. All these letters, Caleb. How can it be possible?"

He didn't answer, and suddenly she didn't want him

to. He had warned her that the combination of money and sex was a powerful lure. She supposed it was too much to hope that the majority of these messages would be from men who really just wanted to father a child. Caleb was most likely right about her not wanting to open these in front of strangers.

"Take me home now," she suggested. "I'll make lunch. Then we'll see what we have."

He gathered up the stack of letters. She couldn't help thinking that every one of those letters was from a man who had agreed to have sex with her sight unseen, either because she had offered money or for some other reason.

A slight shiver went through her.

Caleb stopped and gazed down at her. "You don't have to go through with this. You could stop without ever reading any of these."

She could go on as she had been for the past few years. And she could be alone for the rest of her life with no child to hold in her arms, no baby to love and accept unconditionally.

"Surely one will be all right," she said. "There must be one good man with good intentions." She wished she didn't sound so pathetic.

And suddenly Caleb shifted all the mail to one arm. He cupped her chin in his other palm and tipped her head up, so that she was staring right into his eyes. "I hope you find what you're looking for, Victoria," he said softly, "but if any of these men hurt you, I will personally cut them to pieces. And I don't mean that I'll do that with the power of the press, either. I promise you that I'll lay hands on any jerk that steps out of line. This is Renewal, Victoria. You're not alone here."

And then he kissed her to seal the bargain.

A stack of mail lay on Victoria's kitchen table. She was looking at it as if she were afraid to touch it and yet Caleb knew he couldn't talk her out of her plan. Victoria wanted a baby so much that she had opted to put herself at risk and step way outside her comfort zone.

The fact that she had dressed in red for him was enough to tell him just how far she would go to achieve her goal, and all he had done so far had been to try to discourage her. That wasn't right.

And so he reached out as if to pull a letter from the stack. Nearby Bob paced back and forth on his perch, looking at Caleb like a fretting father who wanted to let loose and swear. "Don't say it," Caleb told the bird. "I'm not going to hurt her."

"Bob," Victoria admonished in a soothing voice. "It's fine. Let me take you into the other room."

Caleb felt a moment of anger. When she brought her prospective father figure here to make love, *if* she actually brought him to her house, who would be there to look out for her best interests except for one small frustrated parrot?

"Shh, Victoria, leave him as he is. He's fine," Caleb told her, brushing her hand with his own. "He's just nervous because he doesn't know me. Who can blame him?"

"You're sure you don't mind?" He could tell by the anxious look she turned to the bird that she loved the reprobate old parrot with a rare depth of feeling.

The bird stared at him as if he didn't trust him one bit. For some reason that made Caleb feel a bit better. "I think Bob and I are going to see eye to eye eventually," he said. "Just give him time. Let him stay."

Victoria visibly relaxed. She took a deep breath and hazarded a look at the pile of letters.

"What are you thinking?" he asked.

"I don't know. I guess I'm thinking that everything I'm looking for could be in this stack of letters or…"

"Or?"

"Or there could be some pretty unpleasant stuff, too. I *did* think of that, you know. I realize you think I'm incredibly naive and insane to do this, but…"

He brushed his fingers lightly over the back of her hand. "I don't think you're insane. Having a baby means a great deal to you. You're working to fulfill a dream. I just want to make sure that you're safe while you're fulfilling it."

"See, I was right about you," she said. "You're a good man, even if it's not necessary to protect me. I know how to steer clear of the bad guys." Then she turned her attention back to the letters. He could almost see her take a deep breath.

"Do you want me to read these to you?" he asked.

Slowly she shook her head. "No, I'm not a coward."

He smiled. "You're anything but that. I think you've proven that already."

"Thank you," she said primly and she pulled the first letter toward her. Carefully she used a letter opener to slit the envelope, the sound of tearing paper breaking the silence. She glanced down at the letter. To say her face blanched would be an understatement. Her eyes suddenly looked twice as large in her pale face.

Immediately Caleb reached for the piece of paper, but she set it aside.

"We'll just skip that one," she said very firmly and she opened another. And another. The first seven went into the same stack. Caleb could only imagine what they said.

Finally on the eighth try, Victoria let out a slow breath. Her shoulders relaxed slightly. "Maybe this one," she said. And to Caleb's surprise, she looked at him as if she wanted to ask him something. She slowly handed him the letter.

"Dear Future Mom," the letter read,

I am a man in my middle years. My life has been fine, but I would like to do something more meaningful. Making a child would, I think, be meaningful, even though I don't really have any time or money to give to being a dad. So your letter seemed to speak to me. I am a man of high intelligence, an accountant who has no bad habits or noticeable physical infirmities to pass on to future generations. I am clean in mind and habit, and I think I would like to consider this further. Please feel free to contact this list of references.
Yours truly, Jeb Marcusson

"What do you think?" Victoria asked, her voice soft and quiet. She has a pretty voice, was the first thought that came into Caleb's mind. He wondered why he had never noticed and why he had never taken the time to talk to her before.

And what did he think? He thought that Jeb's letter made him angry. Maybe because the man wanted to have a child just to add another tally mark to his list of accomplishments. That wasn't Victoria's motivation at all. He'd seen her with Allie MacAllister. Victoria had a heart filled with caring. This wasn't about adding up points for her. He was pretty darn sure Jeb was an egotist who would feel that he was doing the world a favor by passing on his genes. But at least the man hadn't made any indecent comments or insulted Victoria.

"What I think is that you should read through the whole pile and then take a good long time to think before you do anything more," he said. "But you don't have to do all of that today. This could be overwhelming."

She smiled suddenly and her brown eyes lit up. "Thank you. You're very…I don't know…gallant," she said suddenly.

"Gallant?"

She shrugged. "I suppose that's not a word that the press uses very often. Not objective enough. Too old-fashioned, perhaps, but it fits."

"Don't let Denise hear you calling me that," he said with a grin. "She tells me I'm a bear with a sore paw and an annoying growl when we're behind schedule. She's right."

"A bear?" She laughed, and it was a delightful sound, soft and pretty. She could charm men with that laugh. She could charm Jeb, who probably would be too busy noting his own accomplishments to notice. But then, how many people *had* noticed Victoria's lovely laugh? Caleb wondered. He certainly hadn't. He had looked right through her, right past her for two whole years.

"A bear," he admitted, catching up the conversation. "With an extremely bad attitude."

She was still smiling and he wanted to go on saying things to make her smile. He leaned closer.

And suddenly her smile disappeared.

"Heavens, I haven't even fed you like I promised to." She got up and began bustling around the room.

"You don't have to, Victoria," he said.

"I most certainly do. It's past two o'clock, and the only reason you haven't eaten is because of me."

"I didn't notice the time," he said, not wanting her to feel bad. And the truth was that he hadn't noticed. He'd been too preoccupied with her. Funny when he hadn't even paid the slightest bit of attention to her until now.

But now he wanted to know more. Caleb's gaze searched the room. Her kitchen was done in soft blue and yellow and white with light oak accents. It was feminine, much more so than the clothes she wore would lead anyone to suspect. He could see through to the dining and living rooms. Lots of peach and cream, candles and flowers and brass. Her shelves were filled with books. A cute stuffed koala sat on a shelf next to a photo of a man and a woman dressed in theatrical costumes. Who *was* Victoria Holbrook anyway?

He looked at her just as she bent over to pick up something she had dropped. It was the most natural thing in the world to zero in on the sweet rounded curves of her rear. In fact, he couldn't seem to stop himself. He couldn't stop staring. She straightened and began taking things down from a shelf, her arms lifting over her head. Her body was trim and supple.

Heat slid through him. Uncomfortable heat. Raging heat. Caleb stuck one finger inside the collar of his shirt, trying to loosen the damn thing.

"Victoria?" he said.

She stopped and looked at him. "Don't cook for me," he said. "I'd better get back to the office. Denise…"

Victoria gazed at him with wide eyes. Then she nodded. "She'll wonder where you are when she's working hard to keep the bear at bay," she finally said.

"Something like that." It was a lie. Denise was perfectly capable of putting the paper out herself if she had to, and she wasn't even the tiniest bit afraid of him. But if he stayed here, this close to Victoria, all he would be able to think of was what she was planning, how some man was going to remove those prim clothes from her pretty body and take her to bed.

Not him. But if he stayed, if he kissed her one more time or allowed himself one more thought about the curve of her legs or the thrust of her breasts, well…they might both regret the fact that they hadn't kept their distance from each other. If he left now, he could keep things strictly neighborly.

"I'll see you tomorrow," he said. "You'll be all right?"

She nodded. "I'm just going to read through the rest of my mail tonight."

"Of course," Caleb said. She would spend her night curled up in bed with a stack of letters from men who wanted to join her beneath the sheets.

Hell, Caleb thought. And then he looked down at Victoria's innocent face. Virgin eyes, a businesswoman's convictions and a plan that would make any man's body temperature rise to a dangerous level. Who in the world was Victoria Holbrook, anyway?

He didn't know but he intended to find out very soon. It was, after all, the neighborly thing to do.

Chapter Six

Victoria woke up with her face pressed against the kitchen table. A huge stack of crumpled paper lay next to her hand, the throwaways from her night of reading her mail. A pile of just three letters was carefully stashed beneath a copy of *A History of the Westward Journey.* She blinked and stared at the three letters, trying not to remember what types of things had been written in the rejected missives, although the phrase "show you a good time if you raise your price" seemed to flash behind her eyeballs. She hoped Caleb never found out about that one.

The memory of how he had looked when he entered her store yesterday made her breath catch. She had been focussing intently on Allie, a total sweetheart, and yet she had been instantly aware of him when he had walked through the door.

A frown creased Victoria's forehead. "Stop it," she told herself.

"Stop it," Bob mimicked.

"You, too, big guy," she said to him. "Caleb Fremont is a very nice man, an upstanding member of the community and a great writer. That's all he is to us now that we've changed our course."

"Caleb," Bob said. "Big guy."

"Yes, well he certainly is that," she added, trying not to think of Caleb's broad shoulders or the way his muscled body had felt when he had pulled her close and given her that quick hard kiss to seal their bargain. "And we're going to make sure he knows that we don't need him to look after us anymore. I have things well in hand and I should never have involved him in the first place. That was ridiculous to think that Caleb would want to father our child when he obviously could have fathered one any number of times if he had wanted to." And with women who were much more beautiful than she was. The memory of how she had tried to make herself sexy and seduce Caleb made her want to run and hide in a dark room somewhere.

She gestured toward the three letters. "That was a stupid idea I had, but it doesn't matter, anyway. In only a matter of days I might be connecting with Jeb, Donald or Lloyd, and that will be the end of things. Caleb needn't be involved at all."

She felt a slight twinge at that. "It's a good twinge," she told her parrot.

Bob, uncharacteristically, didn't say anything.

But when the doorbell rang he began screeching. "Hellfire hellfire! Caleb! Caleb!"

Victoria's heart slammed into some part of her body it wasn't supposed to slam into. She looked down. Yes, she really was wearing her mother's ancient turquoise and metallic gold bathrobe with the dancing harem girls on it. She had started wearing it after her parents had died and somehow she had never stopped. It had a hole right over the heart. Her mother always joked that it was where Cupid had shot his arrow. Victoria had hated that. It was so sentimental and her mother had always laughed loudly at it, and most of the time she had been in the center of a big crowd when she'd said it. Victoria didn't know why she continued to wear the ratty old thing.

What's more, she had more hip and breast than her mother had had. What had looked cute on her mother looked… Well, it didn't look right on her even if it felt right.

The doorbell rang again.

"Caleb!" Bob screeched. It almost sounded like a plea for help.

The doorbell was replaced with pounding. "Victoria, are you all right?"

Victoria shot Bob a murderous look. She pulled back the door. "Hello, yes, I'm fine. Bob's just antsy today," she said on a breath as she folded her arms over her waist, trying to minimize the sight of what she was wearing.

She looked up into Caleb's eyes and caught the amused look on his face.

"What?" she asked.

"You look…disheveled," he said.

"It's early." She knew she sounded cross.

He chuckled. "I wasn't complaining. It suits you." He reached out and touched a stray curl. It was just hair, no nerves, no sensation. So why did she feel the touch down to the tips of her bare toes? Victoria shivered.

"Can I help you?" she said hurriedly, hoping he hadn't noticed her reaction to his nearness.

He shook his head and stepped in, closing the door behind him. Now he was even closer. "I just wanted to make sure you made it through the night all right."

Victoria laughed and looked back at him. "I'm here. Still alive."

"You know that isn't what I meant." He glanced beyond her to the table.

"Good news," she said quickly, turning and swiping the big pile of crumpled letters into the wastebasket next to the table. "I've decided on three men. I think any one of them might be able to do the trick."

"Trick?"

"Contribute to my baby's gene pool."

Caleb's jaw hardened. "Let me see." He held out his hand as if she was going to hand him the letters.

But she had seen the frown when he had read Jeb's letter. Victoria was beginning to think that Caleb might be a bit old-fashioned in his protective attitude toward women.

"No, it's fine," she said, shaking her head. "In fact, I'm very sure I've made a match." Though she had not been remotely certain of that last night. These letters had been slightly promising, nothing more.

"You've found the perfect man to be the father?"

No, she hadn't. "Yes, I think so."

Caleb gazed down at her, right into her eyes, right

into her soul it seemed. As if he could read her and tell if she was lying. And if he knew that, where would she be? Her conscience would insist that she tell the truth and everything would be spoiled. Because she couldn't go back now and there was nowhere else to go. The man she really wanted to help her wasn't a choice.

"You're sure?" he asked, and his voice seemed to sink right into her. She breathed him in, she remembered how his lips felt against hers. She was this close to being able to guess how it would feel to have the rest of his body naked and against her.

Stepping back quickly, Victoria bumped into the table. She snatched the letters from the table and clenched them in her fist. "Yes," she managed to say. "As a matter of fact, I was just waiting until it was late enough to call each of them. I'm going to see if I can set up a meeting today."

"Where?"

She blinked. "Does it matter?"

"You're meeting a man…no, three men you've never seen in your life and you ask if it matters where you meet them?"

"Oh, that. Yes, of course, I'll make it a public place. Not here, though. Dalloway. Mavis's Kitchen, I suppose." He couldn't argue with that. Mavis's was big and airy and crowded. "Caleb, I don't want to be your responsibility." For some reason she couldn't understand, it was painful to think of Caleb feeling responsible for her. "What I asked you to do the other day was wrong. I…I regret it now." She pulled her robe more tightly about her body.

Caleb blinked. "I suppose I am being a bit of an overbearing jerk."

And against all the warnings that her brain was screaming, breaking every rule she had erected over the course of many years, Victoria reached out and touched his hand. "You're being kind. You're being a good neighbor. You're worrying about me when a lot of men would have run away the other day."

He smiled and shook his head. "I can guarantee you that most men would have jumped you and asked questions later."

She felt heat flood her body. Not her face, she was sure. She did not blush ever, but it felt like a blush. Still, she couldn't allow him to continue to guard her. She had spent years learning to be strong, but it was clear as anything that Caleb had a tendency to make her weak. So she had to break free and run back to a safer path.

"I have to do this on my own, Caleb. Believe me."

"I never meant to insult you," he said gently, taking her hands. "It's obvious that you've succeeded in your life and business without anyone's help."

She looked down at her fingers lying against his skin and savored the feeling of touching him, because in just a second she was going to end it. "I don't know how successful I've been, but I've always tended to follow my own path," she conceded. "Now and then, it's created problems."

Caleb nodded. He released her. "You won't find me criticizing. I've been a bit of a rebel myself with rules that people don't always understand." He smiled at her and she smiled back.

"Like no women from Renewal," she said.

"Exactly. That one stumps people, but I stand by it

anyway. Guess I can't push you then, Victoria. You deserve to follow your own drummer. Just…"

She looked up and waited quietly.

"Just be careful and promise you'll come to me if you need a friend."

She nodded, hot tears gathering and misting her eyes. Her family had traveled around. She had not had friends as a child. Even now she didn't have many. "I'll do that. Thank you."

He turned to go, then turned back. "One more thing."

"Yes?"

And he bent slightly. He placed his lips right over the hole in her bathrobe. It seared the flesh of her breast. "Don't ever open the door wearing this again. You look far too enticing. I almost asked you to let me be the one."

And then he stepped out the door and Victoria stood there, her hand over her breast, her heartbeat pounding frantically against her palm.

It was definitely going to be difficult to switch from the thought of sleeping with Caleb to sleeping with any other man. She wondered how she would manage to submerge her reservations long enough to make a child.

And how would she feel seeing Caleb drive off to other towns to seek his pleasure? For the rest of her life she would know he was with other women while she raised another man's child.

Caleb paced the floor of his office. He had seen Victoria drive off an hour ago. She'd been wearing her usual black and white, but there had been a pale blue scarf at her throat. To identify herself to a stranger, he supposed, for he had no doubts about where she had gone. Had he only imagined that she had looked slightly scared as she had climbed into her car?

Caleb's hands twisted on the piece of paper he was holding. He had wanted to go with her, to sit near to make sure she was all right, but he had promised to stay out of it, and he had to respect her wishes. She would not appreciate a man crowding her, and after all, wasn't that the very thing he had run from all his life? The threat of overwhelming another person, of being overwhelmed by another person? So when she had told him that she had to do this on her own, he had quelled his objections and kept silent. But that had been yesterday when they had been talking theory.

Caleb started toward the door and then stopped. "She asked you not to," he said. "Leave her alone."

He forced himself to sit down and stare at the screen on the computer. The words on the screen seemed to rearrange themselves and disappear. Instead, he saw Victoria staring up at him, adorable with her hair in disarray and that lovely expanse of bare skin over her heart tempting him to touch and taste.

"Hell," he said, slamming his palm against his desk.

"Yeah, I know what you mean," Denise said. "I hate it when the Internet is this slow. Makes me want to chew glass. But what can you do?"

"Nothing, Denise," Caleb said. "Sometimes you just can't do a damn thing."

Jeb Marcusson was…well he seemed a bit oily, Victoria thought. He had big wet lips and he was balding, the remaining hair on his head slicked back and greasy. But that wasn't what she meant. He kept looking at her cleavage, or rather the place where she would have had cleavage if she had been wearing a lower-cut jacket.

He was talking to her about his dreams and his goals and relating his accomplishments, but his gaze was glued firmly to her chest.

"I have my own firm and a boat in Burnham Harbor in Chicago," he was saying, his tongue sliding over his lower lip.

Somehow Victoria managed not to shudder. She supposed it wasn't surprising that the man was assessing her physical attributes since he would have to be somewhat attracted to her to perform.

But she couldn't help choking at the thought. She reached for her water and took a big gulp. She remembered that Caleb had looked at her closely and even intimately once or twice and she had never felt this revulsion.

For a second she hated Caleb for that, for spoiling her for this encounter.

"A boat? That's impressive," she managed to say. She remembered that Jeb had said that he did not have any money to contribute to being a father. Well, lie or not, that was okay. She didn't want anyone but herself to lay claim to her child. She intended to make that a condition of the arrangement.

But when Jeb reached out for his own water glass, she could only imagine him reaching out to touch her and she jumped back. Her water spilled and flooded the table.

"I'm sorry," she said, but Jeb wasn't listening. He had jumped up and was brushing off his pants.

"These just came from the cleaners. They're design-ers," he growled, even though she could tell from the cut that they weren't well made. "You can't get them wet. And I have an appointment in half an hour and no time to change."

And like that, Victoria felt a breath of relief. She reached into her purse and pulled out her wallet. She took out her checkbook and scribbled out a check for one hundred dollars.

"I hope that covers your expenses," she said. "Please don't let me keep you."

Jeb opened his mouth. "Perhaps I was hasty," he said.

But Victoria shook her head. "No, I was," she admitted, rising from the table.

"Wait."

"I'm sorry. This was a mistake," she said, and she picked up the bill and walked away.

Only two to go, she thought as she left. Surely one of them would be right. And suddenly she very badly wanted to report success to Caleb. Who knew why?

Silly woman, she thought. You know why you want to tell Caleb you've got things under control.

There had been those incidents when she had humil-iated herself trying to be what her parents and the boys at school seemed to want. Then four years ago she had met Victor Ayers, who had professed to love her just as she was…until she overheard some of his friends talk-ing about how he had bet he could get the boring ice queen into bed and inspire some passion in her. Finally she had understood. She just wasn't built for relation-ships. Now she wanted the world, and especially Caleb, to know that she was just fine on her own. He was worried about her, the way a friend would worry about another friend. That was the last thing she wanted from him.

Moreover, she wanted to be impervious to need and desire.

And yet, driving home she remembered his lips against her bare skin through the robe, and desire crept in against her will.

Oh, well, at least Caleb would never know. When she saw him next, she fully intended to lie through her teeth.

Chapter Seven

Caleb noticed the minute Victoria made the turn down the main street of Renewal. Good, she was back. At least she was safe. He should just leave it at that. But the next thing he knew, he was walking down the street, holding open her car door, helping her out of her little subcompact.

"Walk with me?" he asked.

"Why?"

"Because if you don't, I'll just have to trail you back to your bookstore and you know what always happens when I do that. Heaven knows what yesterday's book of the day was."

She laughed as he'd meant her to, but it seemed to him that the sound was too soft, somewhat strained. He placed his hand beneath her arm. "How did it go?"

For a minute, he thought she was going to ask what

he was talking about. If she did, he would know that things had gone badly.

"Victoria?"

She turned toward him and looked up at him. "It went…all right for the first round."

"First round?"

She avoided his gaze. "I'll run the ad again."

"Victoria," he drawled, "what happened?"

"Nothing much."

Evasion. Uh-oh. Apprehension lodged within him, making him feel tight and angry. "Define nothing much."

She looked to the side, then slowly turned her gaze back to his with a sigh. "All right, I'll tell you. One of them threw a fit because I spilled water on his pants, one wanted me to up the price and the third…" Her voice trailed off and she got that stubborn look to her chin.

Caleb frowned. "What about the third?"

She blinked.

"Did he touch you?"

"No! But he did keep trying to get my home address."

Caleb's hands clenched into fists. He kept them at his side. She had gone through enough without him worrying her as well.

"For the record, I walked out. I did not tell him where I lived."

"I wouldn't have asked, Victoria," he said, his voice sounding weary. "I have more respect for your intelligence than that."

"Thank you," she said in that prim little voice of hers. "Now I think I should go check in with the bookstore and then I'd like to go home."

She pushed her shoulders back and started to walk down the street. She looked small and sweet and vulnerable, but very intent on being brave. Caleb hated the thought of her going home to an empty house, but she wouldn't want him there, would she?

"Victoria," he said, and she turned and looked back over her shoulder. He walked up to her. "You'll make it happen," he told her. "Your baby."

And he saw the pain in her eyes. "I will," she said. "It's just going to take more time than I thought."

He nodded and let her go. It would take more time and she would be subjected to more strange men who would look at her as if she were a tasty morsel or a meal ticket or a crazy lady to be taken advantage of. She had come home safely today, but what would happen tomorrow or the next day or the one after that?

"Nothing bad," Caleb told himself, but he didn't see how he was going to keep that from happening. Not when she wanted to do everything on her own.

Victoria stared down at the piece of paper in her hand the next day. The copy on this one didn't read much differently from the last one, and yet, something had changed.

"My attitude," she decided. Yes, the last time she had placed an ad in all the neighboring papers, she had been fired up and determined. Now, she was a bit more gun-shy. She hadn't told Caleb, but that last guy had really spooked her. She had found herself sitting across from a very large and scary man and wishing that Caleb were there. Caleb made her feel safe.

"He makes you feel other things, too," she said, and that simple truth put into words made her groan and go back to editing the ad.

Maybe she should just give up her quest to have a child.

She considered that. She rolled it around in her mind. And then she did a simple test. She went to her window and looked outside. Misty was out there playing with her little friends, Rachel and Heather. They were on the swing set in the park, their little-girl shrieks and giggles filling the air, their baby-fine hair streaming out and their feet kicking toward the sky. The sheer wonder of being alive on a magical summer day was written on their faces.

A deep sense of longing crept through Victoria. Thoughts of being able to gaze into a baby's eyes, to share the laughter and tears and dreams of her own child filled her soul. To love a man was to risk too much, but to love a child was to foster joy. She could give what she had never been given, unconditional acceptance.

But she had to have the baby first. Maybe she had just phrased her ad poorly last time…

Victoria looked down at the piece of paper again. She crossed some things out, added some. She dreamed of a baby with silver-blue eyes.

"Aargh! Stop thinking about him. Caleb can't be your lover," she said, her pen skipping across the page in a crazy ark. She was happy that Bob was in the other room. No telling when he might spew that line out for the wrong person to hear.

She went back to her task. And finally she was finished. It was done. She was satisfied.

But she wondered how Caleb was going to react to the changes she had made in her ad.

Maybe he wouldn't even see it…

"Whoa, would you look at this," Denise said later that day. "I wonder who it is that keeps running these things." She shoved the copy under Caleb's nose.

He recognized the writer immediately.

Looking for well-adjusted, genial, mature man interested in creating new life and perpetuating his genetic heritage by fathering a child. Must be healthy, intelligent, clean and free of vices. Marriage not an option, but visitation after birth negotiable. Must provide character/business references. Reply to Future Mom P.O. Box B482, Dalloway, Illinois.

"Hmm, do you know any men interested in perpetuating their genetic heritage?" Denise asked.

No, he didn't, but he knew a naive but lovely woman bent on driving him crazy.

"It's a mystery to me," he said. And it would remain a mystery to the rest of Renewal if he could help it. If he marched down to the bookstore now, Denise would figure out who the mystery writer was. People would hound Victoria, maybe even pity her or laugh at her.

So, no, he wouldn't do that. But he would see her soon. Oh, yes, he would. Visitation negotiable? The very thought of one of these guys showing up after the fact and insinuating himself into her life made Caleb see raging red. What on earth was she thinking?

"Wonder what would make a woman resort to a personal ad to get a daddy for her babies," Denise said.

Caleb blew out a breath. "I imagine she's met a lot of losers in her time and she figures she's better off with a loser she knows for sure won't stay around than one who makes promises he doesn't keep. Obviously she doesn't want a husband."

"Yeah, but why not just ask for the guy to donate sperm for a fee?"

He shrugged. "A guy hard up enough to donate sperm for money might be noble or he might just be a guy who's figured out an easy way to get cash. Might be a con man that knows how to pretend. She might not trust herself to know the difference, and she might not want to have a con artist fathering her child. Maybe she's looking for the right type."

"There's a right type?"

"I guess. She must have decided she at least wanted a man who liked children, who wasn't in it just for the money. Someone with a higher motivation."

"Maybe. Sounds fishy to me. Maybe she's just looking for a roll in the hay or something kinky."

"She is not looking for a roll in the hay." The words came out a bit too hard and rough. Caleb realized he'd made a mistake. He searched for a way to make this right. "A woman who insists that the man be free of vices isn't looking for titillation, definitely nothing kinky."

Denise looked at him hard. She pushed her glasses

up on her nose. "Could be you're right. You probably know more about women than I do, given your vast experience. But if I were her, I'd be careful. Most men don't have your background. Some of them are going to jump to the wrong conclusions. And inviting the guy to show up sometime later to see the kid, that's just…"

"Unthinkable," Caleb said beneath his breath.

"I was going to say unwise."

"That, too," Caleb agreed. "Denise?"

She looked down and waited.

"How old are you?"

His assistant frowned. "Thirty-eight."

He managed not to raise an eyebrow. She was forty-five if she was a day. "I know that you and Jerry decided not to have kids. Do you ever regret it?"

"No," she said quickly, then she shook her head. "Well, that's not exactly right. There are days…you run into a couple with a chubby, giggling little baby in a store or in the park and they look so…so right, so happy…so complete. I don't know. I guess sometimes I do. But then I have Jerry. I'm not alone and we're really not long-term baby people. For us, we made the right choice."

"So it comes down to whether you're a long-term baby person or not?"

"I think so. Why? You're not getting that feeling are you?"

"What feeling?"

"The one that men get that makes them start thinking of making babies with the first available woman."

He took a deep breath. "No, that's not me."

"Okay. For a minute you had that look in your eye like you were considering it. You know that Tarzan thing, that 'I am man, I must spread my seed around' thing. That's the kind of guy that ad we just read appeals to. When that hits the paper, some man will read that and automatically get the urge to throw a female over his shoulder and carry her off to 'make her his woman,' so to speak."

Caleb thought of some man throwing Victoria over his shoulder and making her his woman. Somehow he managed to stay in his seat.

"Denise?" he said.

"I know, let's get the paper out."

"I was going to say thank you for sharing your views with me."

She gave him a look of disbelief.

"Then I was going to ask you to get to work so we could get the paper out."

His assistant laughed and walked away.

He forced himself to stay in the office until the end of the day. It was only after five o'clock that he allowed himself to think of Victoria's plan.

Just how badly did she want a child? And what was she willing to put herself through to get one?

And what was he going to do about the whole thing?

"Nothing," he muttered. No, that was wrong. He was going to do something all right. Probably something tremendously wrong and stupid.

Victoria had only been home for five minutes when her doorbell rang. She opened it to find Caleb standing there, his broad shoulders filling up all the available space in the doorway, his chestnut hair streaked with the sunlight that drifted in behind him. He looked good. He also looked angry.

"Come walk with me," he said, and though his voice was soft, there was no smile on his face.

Come walk with me. A directive. She had never been good with directives, but there was that deeply worried look in his eyes and the fact that she had forced her problems on him when he had just been minding his own business and living his own life.

Carefully Victoria slid her hand into Caleb's and followed him out her door, down the stairs and across the street.

"Where are we going?"

"Somewhere neutral."

"Neutral? Are we going to have an argument?"

He glanced down at her and smiled. "Pistols at sunset," he said.

"I see. I've offended you somehow then."

"Not offended."

"Insulted?"

"Not me. You couldn't say anything about me that most women in town haven't already said."

"If they said bad things, then they didn't know you," Victoria said hotly.

"*You* don't know me, Ms. Holbrook," he said, using the name she didn't like.

The one word was enough to jolt her. "No, I guess I don't. It's just that you've been so nice to me lately…"

He stopped and turned to her. They were standing

outside Gateway Park. "Victoria," he said with a groan.
"I'm sorry, but dammit, I'm…you're making me nuts
with worry. You've been on your own for years, you run
a successful business, you've made a respectable place
for yourself in this town without even trying. You're an
intelligent woman, so…it would seem…hell, it just
stands to reason that you've got to be clear on the basic
fundamentals of dealing with men. I'm sure they come
into your store. I'm sure some of them cause problems
now and then. You know how we are, and by *we* I'm re-
ferring to the male animal. You can't assume you know
a man just because he's nice to you. Men sense that kind
of trust. They use it against you. They use it to get what
they want."

"You wouldn't use my trust against me," she said
with perfect conviction.

He didn't answer. Instead his eyes turned dark and
fierce. "I'm not a saint by any means, Victoria, and anyone in town would tell you that."

She felt herself bristle. "Then I just wouldn't talk
to them."

He laughed at that, a great chortling laugh. "Victoria, I'm very sure you do talk to such people. Every day.
They're your customers, your friends."

She crossed her arms. "Just because you date a lot of
women doesn't mean you're not a good person. Why are
you spending so much time cautioning me?" And then
she widened her eyes as the truth hit her right in the part
of her brain where truth always manages to strike. "You
saw my new ad, didn't you?"

"I'm the owner and editor. If it goes in, it goes past me."

"Hmm, I knew I shouldn't have posted it in the *Gazette,* but it was on the first list and I just didn't think." She held her hands out in an "oh, well" gesture.

"For the record, just how long was that list?" His voice was very low and very quiet, but cold, more cold than Victoria could remember.

"Not too long." She freed her hand and started to walk away.

"How long exactly, would you say?" He matched her steps, the two of them passing beneath the black wrought-iron arch at the park's entrance and moving down one of the hedge-lined pathways.

"Twenty newspapers. Or so," she said, trying not to flinch in anticipation of his reaction.

"Twenty newspapers?" Caleb stopped dead in his tracks. He took both of Victoria's hands in his own and turned her to face him. "Twenty newspapers? Is that how many you sent it to the first time?"

"No." Her fingers felt small in his grasp, but in a good way. She was very aware of the difference between the sexes at this moment, her small size to his large one, her softness to his steel. Looking up into his eyes, she wanted to lean closer, to place her head on his chest and ask him to help her figure out how to make everything work out the way she'd planned. But that would have been weak, and weak wasn't her way. "The first time, I only sent it to half as many places. I just…I just wanted to move things along, to get things over with. To get past this part."

"Victoria, listen to yourself," he said, and his voice grew warmer. He touched her cheek. "You don't want to do this. Really. You don't want to give yourself to a stranger."

And the truth was that no, she didn't, but her dreams were slipping away. She had already waited too long in a vain attempt to pretend that life would simply happen to her, that opportunities would drop into her lap.

"Don't go to Dalloway again," Caleb told her.

"I have to. I have to take the next step to get to the final one."

Slowly he shook his head. He tugged on her hands and she tumbled against him. "No," he said. "You don't. We'll work this out. I'll help you."

Victoria froze in his arms. She pressed her face into his shoulder. "What do you mean?" she mumbled, her breath catching.

She could feel him take a deep breath. For a while he was silent as if he didn't mean to speak at all. Then he blew out his breath in a long whoosh. "I mean what you think I mean."

A sudden vision of herself and Caleb somewhere in another town where he had taken countless women before her rose up. But he had taken those women to bed because he wanted to, because he craved them, because they lit a fire deep within him. When he slept with those women it was an act of pure lust, not charity. And suddenly she pulled back far enough to look up into his eyes. "You're thinking about doing this out of pity, aren't you?"

He laughed then, an awful hoarse laugh. "Victoria, if there is one thing I can guarantee you, it's that pity doesn't have a damn thing to do with this."

"Then why?"

He hesitated. "To be honest, I don't actually know. Or at least I don't know completely. I do know that I don't want to see you putting yourself in danger. And I don't want you getting involved in legal entanglements. It's making me insane. I can't work, I'm starting to feel an urge to punch total strangers between the eyes. Did you really mean that when you said that visitation was negotiable? I thought you didn't want that."

"I don't, but after yesterday, I realized that I really didn't want a man who was just doing it for the money. It was so ugly, so dirty and scary. But I figured that if I went the other route, and if the man was really going to impregnate me for some noble reason or for the child, then it wasn't really fair to ask him to simply walk away afterward. In fact, you might have noted that I didn't even mention money this time."

"I did."

"That will get rid of a lot of the less savory types, the ones who have angles."

"Everyone has an angle, Victoria. You have an angle. Be honest."

She considered that. "Yes, I guess I do. But if the man's angle is simply that he wants a child, then I can deal with that."

"If a man wants a child that badly, he might ask too much."

"I'll make him sign a contract."

"Contracts have loopholes. You might end up losing the one thing in life that you want so much that you're willing to risk everything for it. Your baby. That would be worse than never having a child at all."

"It won't happen."

Caleb slid his palm beneath her jaw. "It won't happen if I change my mind and take you up on your original proposal."

Victoria's heart felt as if it were beating slowly and yet so hard she could barely bear it. Caleb's eyes were fierce, his beautiful face stern and set.

"Why would you do that?" she asked. "You said that you couldn't."

"I said I didn't want to. I've changed my mind. I'll do it, and willingly, too. You don't have to run any more ads, you can cancel your post office box and ignore the mail that comes pouring in. I'll be the father of your baby, Victoria, but…"

"But?" Of course, he had an objection. He didn't want to do this, he had been adamant about not being tossed into this situation, but she had dragged him in and now he was agreeing, however reluctantly. He didn't want to do this, but he was. Obviously there would be rules.

"But you have a condition," she prompted.

He smiled slowly into her eyes. He raked his thumb gently over her lower lip, sending sensation spiraling through her. "Oh, I definitely have a condition, Victoria."

Chapter Eight

"I'll need to know what your condition is, and then I'll have to think about it," Victoria said, looking up at him with those earnest, completely honest brown eyes of hers. "This isn't the kind of thing we should jump into."

A long laugh escaped Caleb. "If I remember correctly, you were poised to do a swan dive into this situation just days ago."

"I was. I didn't know you then. I didn't really care about your end of things. Now I do."

"Because you think I'm nice."

"That and the fact that you've gone out of your way to help me even though there was no reason for you to do so."

"I had reasons," he said, but he realized he wasn't quite sure what they were. Partly it was because he remembered how vulnerable his mother had been when she'd come up against his father, but that was only a small part of things. "I have reasons for offering to do this now." But what in hell were they?

"Tell me." Her words were practically a whisper.

"There are two lives at stake here, yours and your child's."

"And the man's," she added.

"And the man's," he agreed, although he didn't want to think about the men she had been soliciting.

"So you're doing this to protect me and my baby."

"Partly."

"What's the rest?"

He shrugged. "Maybe I'm tired of taking social trips to Dalloway."

She froze at that. "I wouldn't stop your trips to date women in Dalloway."

"You will if we agree that I'm going to father your baby."

"I don't understand."

He edged in closer. "If we do this, Victoria," he said, taking her chin in his hand, "we're going to do it right."

"Right, as in…"

"Married." He said the word as if it had just popped into his head. Maybe it had, but he knew that he meant it.

"Married! You don't want to be married! *I* don't want to be married."

"When I said that, what I meant was that I don't want someone who expects love in the traditional sense."

"Neither do I."

"Other than that I have no real objection to the basic

concept of two people joining together for companionship and in a common cause. I can't think of a better cause than having a baby, can you?"

"You don't think I can raise a child on my own?"

"I know you can. That's not my problem with the situation."

"What is?"

He led her to a bench. "You told me that you wanted to do this right and regular, all the way. Well, normally a baby isn't conceived by two total strangers who come together for one night just to make a baby and then the father figure fades into black. What will you tell your child years later when he asks? He's bound to ask."

"I'll tell him the truth."

"Even if it hurts? Even if it makes him or her feel forever different from the rest of the world?"

And she stopped at that. "I hadn't thought of it that way."

"I hadn't, either, not at first. But then I remembered once, when my parents were having one of their fiercest arguments, a horrendously bad one, wondering why I couldn't have a normal family. It was what I wanted most in the world at the time."

"But you gave that up."

He lifted one shoulder. "The price seemed too high."

"And yet you're proposing that we marry."

He managed a small smile. "You don't ask all that much of a man, Victoria. I figured I might do."

"And what would you get out of this situation?"

"Maybe I just want to patch up my reputation. Won't

everyone be surprised when I get married, and to a Renewal woman, no less?"

Victoria rolled her eyes. "That's not much of a reason."

"Then how about this? I get to give a child my name, a head start in life and a chance at a perfectly normal life. I get to leave behind something more than my newspaper. There are many men who don't ever get that opportunity. Maybe you're giving me a chance to do something lasting and honest. And after all, you and I are a good match. Neither of us wants love."

She gazed at him solemnly. "I'm not sure I can accept."

"It's a condition I won't waver on. A child should know that his dad wasn't paid to father him. Every child should know that he was the conscious choice of both parents."

"You're still worried that I'm going to get hurt, physically or otherwise by some man. You're trying to make sure that doesn't happen."

"I won't hurt you, Victoria," he said. "That's a promise." And he realized she was right. Here was a chance to protect. This time he wasn't helpless and he didn't have to offer more than he was capable of giving.

She rose on her knees on the bench and she cupped her hands around his face.

"You are a noble man."

He opened his mouth to protest, but she touched her fingers to his lips. "I'll agree with your proposal, then, but…"

"But you have a condition."

"Only one," she promised. "After our child is conceived, we end the marriage."

He frowned, but she shook her head.

"We have to. I don't want to be married, not even to a man like you, and you don't really want to be married, either, do you?"

"I didn't ask you out of pity, Victoria."

"I know. You asked me out of friendship."

He slid his arms around her.

"What are you doing?" she asked, and he felt her shiver beneath his hands.

"If we do this, Victoria, we'll have to do more than be friends. You know that, don't you?"

"Of course, yes. I know."

"Do you really want to trust your body to a total stranger?"

She tried to turn her head. He gently nudged her back. "Look at me, Victoria."

She did, and he could see that she was frightened, even though he knew she would never admit it.

"No." It was probably the hardest *no* she had ever uttered. He'd just bet that Ms. Victoria Holbrook didn't admit to uncertainty very often.

"I don't want you to make love to a stranger, either. I don't want you to have to begin this on an unpleasant or frightening note."

"But you don't really want to be married. You would have said as much only yesterday, or at least the day before."

"Well, you've got me there, Victoria. I've uttered that phrase too often to take it back now. Everyone, including you, would know I was a liar."

For some reason that seemed to relax her. "So this doesn't have to be permanent," she reasoned. "We can get married, start our baby off right and then end things amicably."

"It sounds almost simple," he agreed.

"No regrets later for either of us. No risks," she added.

"It would seem not."

"And we could save your reputation," she said with a chuckle.

He frowned at her. "Which one, the real one that says I'm an untamed womanizer or the good guy one you're always trying to pin on me?"

"Hmm, it seems that you might be left with both. Because you're a good guy, you're marrying a woman from Renewal to protect her and help her fulfill her dearest dream, and then you'll go back to your 'no Renewal women' rule. Nothing really needs to change, does it?"

She looked up at him with longing in her eyes.

He knew that things would change, and maybe not for the better. She probably knew it, too. These few days when they had been friends would never come again. When this was over, they could not go on as they had. They would have a child in common. But if he let that stop him, she'd go back to Dalloway.

"Nothing has to change," he agreed. "So you'll marry me?"

She gazed at him solemnly, studying him as if to see into his soul. He wondered what she really saw when she looked at him.

"It seems like cowardice to take this way out."

"You were going to make love with me before."

"Because it was simple."

He laughed. "Victoria Holbrook, I don't think anything where you're concerned could ever be simple."

She frowned. "You're probably right. My parents always told me that, anyway. So...coward or not, and I *am* a coward—I can confess now that the thought of making love with a stranger petrifies me—I say yes, Caleb. We'll do this your way. You agree to end things after we're sure I've conceived?"

He raised his right hand. "I promise."

She shook her head. "I'll have my attorney draw up a contract. Some man told me once that I had to be wary of loopholes. I want to make sure this goes right. I don't want you doing anything noble when this is over."

He groaned. "Victoria, stop telling people I'm noble. It's bad for my reputation."

She laughed, a lovely sound. "Think what having a child will do to it."

"Ah, you're wrong there, Victoria. Women flock to men with small children."

She punched him. "So this is all a trick to make yourself more appealing to the ladies."

"You've found me out."

"Yes," she said. "I have. When will we do it?"

He almost choked. A sudden picture of Victoria coming to him in a black lace negligée that hid very little of her perfect skin rose up in his mind. He peeled away the small bit of lace with his teeth, and she smiled and came into his arms. "Um, when will we do it?"

"Caleb! I meant when will we get married?"

"Oh, that. As soon as it's legally possible, I suppose.

There's no point in waiting, given the circumstances. And then we'll do it," he said with a grin.

"We'll make a baby," she said, crossing her arms.

But he knew they would do much more than make a baby. They would make some serious heat. Victoria was going to know that her child was conceived in a moment of passion, the way all children should begin.

And he was going to be able to sleep peacefully tonight, not worrying about some man taking advantage of her.

Other than himself, of course. He felt a slight twinge of guilt. Because while he wanted to help Victoria achieve her dream, he also very definitely wanted to lie with her naked body wrapped around his.

And he knew that that wasn't what had compelled her to agree to the match.

The wedding was small and private, because neither of them wanted a lot of fanfare. In fact, they wanted no fanfare at all, but somehow the word had got out, Victoria realized, when Denise, Caleb's assistant, stepped into the small chapel bearing a disposable camera.

"I'm sorry," Caleb said. "I should have told you that I'd mentioned our wedding to Denise. It's bound to come out sooner or later, and if it comes out later, it will look as if something's not quite right. Denise is under strict orders to be tactful in her gossiping. She can do that when she tries."

Victoria couldn't help smiling at Caleb's tone. Everyone in town knew that Denise spilled secrets right and left, but they also knew that she was devoted to her boss. Victoria wasn't too worried. She even turned to smile so that Denise could get a good picture.

"You're probably right," she said to her soon-to-be-husband. But something *wasn't* quite right. She was marrying Caleb Fremont, and Caleb didn't want a wife. No matter what reasons he gave, she knew that she had all but forced him to this. Caleb had a protective streak that he just couldn't overlook. He had been genuinely worried about her sanity and safety, and she couldn't really blame him. She'd known she was playing with fire soliciting men.

It was only the fact that she had promised herself to research the men to death that had enabled her even to go that route.

But in the end, she had still been scared. So she owed Caleb a great deal. Soon she would owe him for more. He was going to give her a child. He was going to take her to bed and do all that was necessary to give her a baby, and she would just bet that he was going to do it really well, too. She only hoped that she wouldn't prove an utter disappointment the way she had so many times in her life.

Victoria trembled beneath Caleb's fingers.

"Are you all right?" he asked. "Do you need to sit down before we begin?"

"No," she said with more vehemence than she had intended. Putting things off wouldn't make her less nervous.

"Smile, hon," Denise said again. "I swear, Caleb, no one, and I mean no one, is gonna believe this. You marrying Victoria, a woman straight from Renewal. I wonder when the two of you got together..."

Caleb turned to his assistant. "You can just wonder, Denise. That's not going to be printed in the newspaper, and it *is* my paper, I hope you remember. So just the basics and a picture of the happy couple." He looked down at Victoria. "The *happy* couple," he said, whispering so close to her ear that his warm breath caressed and sent a shiver down her skin. She knew by his coaxing that she must have looked concerned.

She rose on her toes and placed her mouth near his ear. "Denise is right. No one will believe this wedding. People are either going to wonder what I slipped in your drink, or else they're going to take bets on what I'm holding over your head."

"Let them," he said, whispering back so that his lips nuzzled her skin. "What's between my wife and myself stays between us, and it's nobody else's business. We're getting married today, Victoria, and we've both chosen to do so. For as long as it lasts, it's going to be a real marriage. You understand?"

She nodded, which was a mistake since his lips connected with her neck and she couldn't stifle a small gasp of pleasure.

"Whoo!" Denise said, fanning herself with her hand. "I wish you two would save the heat for after the wedding. This could get embarrassing in a minute."

Caleb smiled down at his bride-to-be. "Don't worry, Denise. We'll wait until tonight." His voice held a hint of promise. Of course, Victoria reminded herself, that was just show for Denise's sake.

"Ready?" he asked.

"As ready as I'm going to get," Victoria said as panic

climbed inside her. Somehow she stumbled forward next to Caleb. Somehow she heard herself repeating the words, "I take this man…"

She would take Caleb and then she would give him back.

In no time at all, she would be back to her old life and he would be back to his. And all they would ever share then would be the child they were going to start making as soon as the sun went down tonight.

Chapter Nine

"You may now kiss your bride," the pastor said, and Caleb drew Victoria into his arms. He stared straight into her eyes and slanted his lips over hers. She leaned slightly forward and into him, one arm looping around his neck as Denise snapped the picture. Her lips were soft, pressed closed. He licked at the seam of her mouth and her eyes flew open, her lips parting slightly before she closed her eyes again.

She was unschooled, probably virtually untouched, he surmised. He would have to treat her carefully, go slowly. But when she rose to nest more comfortably against him and her body leaned against his, his brain stopped functioning. He took her mouth again. And again, savoring the taste of her.

"Caleb, this is a family newspaper." Denise's voice broke in, and Caleb released his wife. Her lips were rosy. She looked as if she might be a bit unsteady on her feet. He slid an arm around her waist and caught the good pastor grinning at him.

"Take care of her, son," the man said.

"I will. Don't print that picture," he told his assistant as he shepherded his wife down the aisle and out the door. What on earth had he been thinking, manhandling Victoria that way? The ceremony only called for a simple peck, not a prelude to full-blown passion.

"I guess they'll believe it's real now, won't they?" his bride asked, her voice still shaky, and Caleb couldn't help laughing.

"It certainly felt real, Mrs. Fremont."

She started and then caught herself. "For now," he thought he heard her whisper. Oh, yes, his sweet, prim little wife didn't really want this marriage. She had made it clear that she would do whatever it took to have a baby. And if that meant letting her husband take liberties in public, she would do that.

For some reason, Caleb's good mood vanished. He and Victoria were legally married, and neither of them really wanted it. Did they?

An hour later, he was pretty certain that the answer, at least for Victoria, was a firm no. They had decided to keep their own houses, since the marriage would be of short duration, but they would temporarily live in his home. As he neared the front door, Caleb scooped Victoria up into his arms.

"Caleb, put me down."

"It's tradition, Victoria," he said with a laugh.

"But we're not really married."

"Sounded legal enough to me."

"It was, but it's not lasting."

"Nothing lasts. But if we're going to pretend, then we'll pretend all the way for the sake of the baby. We've certainly got everyone fooled in town."

"I know. Lindsay Dufray, who is my absolute best customer, was practically leading a cheer when she saw us coming out of the chapel. I have the terrible feeling that she's planning something awkward, like a personal shower."

"Is that one of the ones…"

She avoided his glance. "Yes, the embarrassing ones where they give you revealing underwear. I am not a revealing underwear kind of person." She said it defiantly as if he would judge her based on what she wore beneath her clothing.

"Me, either. I hardly ever wear peekaboo boxers," Caleb said, with a grin.

She laughed. Thank goodness.

"Victoria, I don't want to change you. This isn't going to be that kind of marriage."

"Yes, it isn't going to be a real marriage."

He turned her toward him. "Are you going to be able to go through with…everything?"

"It's awfully late to be worrying about that now," she admitted.

"Not too late, though."

"I know, but…I'm okay," she said. And with that, he carried her over the threshold into their new life. He kicked the door closed behind him and let her slide slowly to the floor and out of his arms.

For a few seconds, they stood there just looking at each other. Caleb didn't know about her, but he was very aware that this marriage had been made for one reason and one reason alone. Consummation. Procreation. They would make love until they made a baby. That was the extent of things.

Victoria looked as nervous as a woman could get.

"I'm not going to jump you," he said.

"You're not?"

"At least not now."

"When?"

"When the time is right. When the mood is right."

"What if it never is?"

He thought of her in that red dress. He thought of her leaning into him for that kiss at the church.

"Believe me, it will be right. Very soon, but perhaps it would be better if we get to know each other first, if we pretend that this is a real marriage and try to be comfortable with each other and with our new roles."

"All right, then." She took a step back and seemed to relax slightly.

"All right." A squawking voice broke in. Victoria whirled. Bob was on his perch in a big new cage in the corner.

"You brought him?" she asked her husband.

"I know you asked Misty and her mom to look after him until Monday when you were moving your things, but I thought you might miss him. He's family, after all, isn't he?"

"All I've got," she said, gazing up at her husband.

"Oh, I wouldn't say that. Temporarily you have a husband," Caleb told her.

"And you have a wife," she pointed out, but Caleb thought that her voice sounded a bit faint.

To say that Victoria was nervous was to understate the obvious. She was practically twisting knots in her fingers. She could barely walk and talk and think. What should she do? She had somehow initiated this marriage by stirring up Caleb's protective urges. Now she needed to free him from his bondage as soon as possible, but what should she do? Should she suggest that he take her to bed? Should she let him know in that way that she was eager to set him free as soon as she could? Would he understand or would he simply think she was like most women, eager to make love with him?

And she would be lying to herself if she didn't admit that she found Caleb highly attractive and desirable. But she didn't want him to think that she had ulterior motives here. She didn't. She would never have suggested this marriage or pursued him, and, besides, she was way out of his class. She didn't know the first thing about pleasing a man or seducing a man or even much beyond the basics she had read about. Sex with her was bound to be awkward, maybe even tedious for a man of Caleb's passionate tastes.

So although she was eager to let him know that she wasn't going to stretch this marriage out, she was also petrified of the night to come.

Her thoughts whirled through her head. Caleb touched her shoulder.

She jumped.

"I'm sorry," she said on a gasp. "I just—it's just—"

"Come on," he said, and he took her hand and led her into the next room. It was a large den with dark leather couches and birch occasional tables. He flipped on some music.

"You're putting me in the mood?" she asked.

Caleb laughed. "Yes, for chess." He directed her to an exquisite mahogany game table with game pieces resembling statues of men.

"They're the titans of publishing," he said. "Hearst, McCormick and so on. A custom job from a friend."

"A woman friend?"

He laughed. "I do have friends who aren't women."

"Maybe, but it's usually women who think up these kinds of clever little ideas. I see it all the time in the store. Women are always coming in and custom-ordering some rare tome for their husband or significant other. Of course, men rarely give books as gifts, at least the men who shop at Timeless Publications."

"Hmm, are you stalling, Victoria?"

"Stalling?" Her voice squeaked.

"I don't mean stalling about making love, sweetheart. Do you know how to play chess or not?"

Just as he'd hoped, that stubborn little chin rose. "Of course I play chess. I have dual degrees in literature and mathematics. You're on, Caleb."

Thank goodness. If she hadn't played chess, he didn't know what he would have suggested next. The truth was that he didn't really know his wife any better than she knew him. And he wanted her to feel comfortable in his presence. He wanted her to be able to concentrate on something other than their marriage project, the process of making a baby.

"You're good," Caleb said a short time later.

"So are you." She sounded slightly surprised.

"It's a hobby I took up at a young age. I like activities that deal in precision."

"It figures. No emotion."

"Shut up and play, Victoria."

She laughed. "Oh, so you're a testy player."

"I'm a ruthless player." He took one of her bishops.

"I'm a take-no-prisoners player myself," Victoria said, knocking off one of his knights.

"Chess is all science and math," he mused.

"It's mechanical," she added. "You can play chess at a distance, by mail or over the Internet."

"And yet," Caleb said, "it's a game that has inspired passion." He took his wife's queen.

Victoria looked up, aghast. "You distracted me," she accused, her voice woeful. "I deserved that." And then she brushed her hand through her hair. She leaned forward over her hands, and Caleb noted the shadowed V of the navy dress she had donned. He wondered what she would say if he leaned over the table and placed his lips there.

Victoria took his other knight. "Not nearly as good as a queen, but it will have to do."

Caleb looked down at the board. "Did you do that on purpose?" he asked. "To distract me, too?"

"What?" she asked, and he realized that she wasn't bluffing. She had been so intent on the game that she hadn't even noticed that he was staring at her cleavage. He stared at it now.

And now she noticed. He could tell because her breathing grew deeper. Her lashes fluttered. She gripped the edge of the table. He was making her nervous. No, more than nervous. Scared. Damn! Well, what had he expected? She had told him she had virgin genes, and she knew very well that he did not. She must be in a state of panic thinking that the inevitable was getting closer.

"I think this game is over," he said softly.

"We're not done yet," she insisted. "You haven't beaten me yet."

"I'm not sure I *can* beat you. Anyway, it's late."

And he saw when she realized the inevitable. "Yes, I guess…I guess we should go to bed."

"Yes, I think we should."

Caleb led her to the room they would share and put her bag down next to the bed. "I'll give you time," he said softly.

Victoria nodded nervously and he left her. When he returned a few minutes later, she was lying on the bed, a sheet pulled up to her neck.

He wanted to smile tenderly, but he was afraid that he would offend her.

Instead, he simply clicked off the lights, removed his robe and slid into bed beside her. His hand accidentally touched her leg. She was wearing something soft and slick. Silk over the silk of her flesh, he couldn't help thinking, holding back a groan.

"Victoria?" he asked.

"Y-yes." She cleared her throat. "Yes?"

"I'm going to put my arm around you," Caleb told her. "And then we're both going to sleep."

She sat up in bed. It was dark but there was moonlight sifting in through the window shades. He could see her outline. The thought that she was naked beneath that silk made breathing difficult. "I'm not a coward, Caleb. I can do this."

"I would never call you a coward, Victoria. I know you're not, and I'm sure you can do this." But he wanted her warm and willing, not just determined. He wanted her to feel safe with him before he touched her intimately. "But for tonight, let's just lie together. Let's take it slow. I married you because I didn't want you to make love to a stranger. I don't want to be a stranger in your bed."

"It's your bed," she reminded him.

"It's our bed."

"Yes, all right."

"So…I'll hold you," he said, and he covered the space between them. He took her in his arms. She trembled. He barely kept breathing. He didn't know how he would get through the night.

"Are you all right?" Caleb managed to ask.

"I'm…I'm good." Her voice was so soft and strained he could barely make out the words.

"That's okay, then. Good night, Victoria." He wondered if he was insane to be turning away from what she had offered.

"Good night, Caleb. And…thank you." Her words confirmed what he had suspected. She wasn't really ready to join her body with a man's, not even a man she knew.

And so he settled against her. He closed his eyes and waited for the dawn. He didn't expect sleep, not with Victoria held against him this way, but he did hope that if they lay this way long enough, she would relax and sleep herself.

And so the night began.

Victoria lay there in the dark, feeling as if her body was on fire. Caleb's arms were about her, his side pressed to hers. She could feel his warm breath against her hair.

He was naked. He was beautifully naked. She could tell even though she didn't dare move a finger or even a muscle. If she woke him, she might…she might do anything. She might even ask him to make love with her, and he so clearly was having to psych himself up for the moment.

The thought made her squirm with humiliation.

Caleb shifted in bed. Darn, she had very nearly awakened him then.

But it was so hard lying still. Why had he married her? she couldn't help wondering. But she knew the answer. She had all but forced him to it by her reckless behavior. She should never have allowed Caleb to get involved in her personal problems. She had been doing fine on her own.

Oh, who was she kidding? She had not been doing fine. That was why he had gotten involved in the first place, because she had grown desperate and jumped off into water over her head.

Caleb had tried to save her. He had sacrificed the single life he loved so that she could safely have a child. And now he was going to have to make love to her until he gave her a baby. How must he feel about that? He who could sleep with any woman he wanted to?

Victoria squirmed again. She wasn't sure how long she could do this. Caleb was such a good man. To drag this on too long just wouldn't be right.

Maybe…it was dark. Maybe if he pretended she was someone else. Maybe now while he was warm and sleepy and not quite awake, she could do and say the right things to get him in the mood and get things over with. Surely she would conceive pretty quickly. It was the right time of the month.

The thought made it almost impossible to take even one breath. She felt paralyzed, more frightened than she could remember. She remembered throwing herself at Eric Arness in high school and how awful that had been.

But Caleb was asleep. Maybe if she was careful, he wouldn't even wake up completely. Maybe it would be like a dream and he would think he was making love to another woman. Could she pretend to be another woman?

Victoria slowly, so slowly it almost hurt, turned her body. Millimeter by millimeter. She barely breathed. She thought she might die before this was over.

Slowly her front came in contact with Caleb's side. And then yet more slowly, she reached out. Her palm connected with Caleb's chest. He was warm and firm and muscled. He was heaven to touch.

But she couldn't think about that now. Slowly she inched her hand up over his flesh, trying not to think of how wonderful it felt. She leaned over him more fully, her hip touching his. The movement brought her night-gown tight against her. It stretched taut against her chest, the strap slipping down, mostly exposing one breast.

She stopped. She tried to breathe deeply, but her lungs felt as if they were on fire. She was touching Caleb. She moved her palm up one inch farther, and the tip of one finger grazed his nipple.

Suddenly strong arms grasped her waist, lifting her on top of him.

She shrieked.

"Dammit, Victoria, I was trying to keep my hands off you tonight."

"I'm sorry."

"Do you want a baby this bad? All right, then, I'll give you your baby."

He pulled her down and brought her mouth to his in a hard, demanding kiss, an angry kiss. Her head swam. She couldn't think. She didn't want to think, but he was so angry. He didn't understand.

"It wasn't that," she said when he released her for air. "This wasn't about the baby. Not really. I just…I just…I'm sorry."

And he let his breath out on a whoosh. "No, I'm the one who's sorry. Did I hurt you? Did I scare you?"

"No, no," she said, shaking her head hard. "Neither. *I* scared me. I wanted… It's so hard waiting, Caleb. I couldn't sleep. I thought if I touched you while you were sleeping, it would make it easier for you to get used to the thought of making love with me. It wouldn't feel so daunting then."

And suddenly he was chuckling, laughing so hard that he was shaking beneath her.

"You think that I was waiting because the thought of making love with you was distasteful?"

"I know that marrying a woman to give her a baby wouldn't have been on your list of things to do last week."

He touched her cheek. "No, no it wouldn't have, but if you think I don't want you, Mrs. Fremont," he said in a raspy voice, "then think again." And as he raised his hips against her, she could feel the evidence of his desire. "I'm barely holding on."

"Because you thought I was some woman from your dreams."

"I haven't slept a wink. How could I sleep with you beside me clad only in this flimsy bit of silk?" he whispered. "Or should I say barely clad?" And his hand closed gently around her exposed breast.

She gasped.

He took her mouth. He nuzzled his way over her lips and down her throat and then touched her breast with his mouth.

Her whole body reacted. Heat and desire filled her. And then Caleb rolled with her, bracing himself above her. He kissed his way down her throat and lower still until breathing became unimportant. Only his touch mattered.

"You think I don't want you? Well, think again, my wife. I want you, and since you seem to want me as well, then let's have each other."

And he took her in his arms. He made desperate love to her and then gentle love. She learned that she could be wanton and wild and demanding. She learned what true passion was, and she learned to dread the morning.

In the morning, reality would intrude.

"Love me again," she said.

"Gladly," he whispered. And Victoria learned what the women of Dalloway had known for years. Caleb Fremont knew how to please a woman.

And she would have him until she conceived. She wondered if she might have already done so.

Chapter Ten

He had been married to Victoria for three weeks, Caleb realized one morning as he sat at the breakfast table and drank his morning coffee. Three weeks, and panic had not yet begun to set in.

That was because his wife made no demands on him, he thought, staring at her shiny dark hair as she bent over her morning paper. At least no demands other than those related to their baby project, and even there she didn't demand. He was eager to have every inch of her. He wondered what the people of Renewal would say if they realized the hidden passionate depths that lay beneath the surface of their seemingly fussy little bookseller.

"What are you smiling at?" Victoria asked, flipping her paper over as if she would find the answer to her question printed there.

"I was just wondering what the book of the day was yesterday," he lied.

She shrugged. "*Harry Potter.* Since I made the changes to the store, popular fiction has caught up with us."

"A shame," he said. "Not that there's anything wrong with *Harry Potter*. I'm glad that your business is doing so well. I was just beginning to appreciate all those odd little tomes you used to sell."

She smiled back at him, putting her paper down. "I still sell them. I just sell more of the others. If not for Harry, yesterday's bestseller would have been *The Sex Lives of Amphibians*."

"Someone actually wrote a book about that?"

Victoria laughed. "I don't really know. I made that up."

"Mrs. Fremont? Lying?"

Victoria wrinkled her nose. "Stretching the truth. The real book was about amphibians, but nothing so intimate."

"I should hope not. Even amphibians deserve their privacy. Who wants researchers poking about your pond when you're feeling amorous and just want to have a little fun with your wife?"

"You think amphibians think that way?" she teased.

"Could be."

She laughed, a delicious sound. "You're incorrigible."

"Yes, and with all this talk of sex, I'm also very much in the mood to make love with my wife."

"Caleb, we have to go to work."

"We'll go in late."

"What will people think?"

"I hope they'll think that we've only been married for three weeks and we're still blind with lust." And he reached for her, rising to his feet and pulling her flush against his body. She fit him in all the right places, her body warm and curved and soft. He leaned forward and kissed her lips, then dipped lower to nuzzle her neck.

She gasped and leaned into him, wrapping her arms around his waist to keep from falling. "Caleb, you're…"

"Hmm? I'm what?" he asked. "If you want me to stop, say so. In spite of how much I want you, I will. I'll always stop if you say so, Victoria."

His lips touched the tip of one breast. She gasped. "No, I'm…good," she said. "That's what I meant. *You're* good."

And he lifted her into his arms and turned toward the stairs.

The doorbell rang three times in rapid succession.

Victoria exchanged a look with Caleb. "It's only eight in the morning. Who can that be?"

And because the someone at the door continued ringing the doorbell, Caleb gently set his wife down. He went to see who was so eager to gain admittance.

It was Gina Gregory, who subbed at the bookstore on Saturdays. Gina was a junior in high school. She looked up at Caleb with big, worried eyes. "Can I see Ms. Holbrook—I mean, Mrs. Fremont?" she asked. "It's important."

Wasn't everything important when you were seventeen? Caleb thought, remembering his own high school years, but Gina looked genuinely worried, and so he showed her into the kitchen where Victoria had somehow managed to repair her hair and was once again looking like the indomitable businesswoman she was.

"Come in, Gina," she said gently. "Sit down." She

gave Caleb a pleading look and he got the instant message. The girl needed privacy.

Caleb excused himself and headed for the door, but as he was going out, Gina started to cry. "Oh, Mrs. Fremont, I'm pregnant, and I don't know what to do. My folks will hate me if they find out. My father never liked Larry in the first place, and maybe he was right. Larry said that it probably wasn't his baby, but it is. It really is." And she began to sob harder, dropping her head onto her hands.

Caleb couldn't help looking back at his wife. She had moved around the table and gathered Gina close. She held the girl and let her cry, stroking her hair.

Later, from the next room, Caleb heard Gina sniff and then his wife's gentle, quiet voice broke the silence. "I know it seems like the end of the world," she told Gina, "but we're going to find a way to make everything come out right. I promise I'll help you, and we'll do whatever is humanly possible to work through this."

As the words left his wife's lips, Caleb frowned. She might be getting herself into something pretty deep here, something that would come crashing down on her head. But he knew enough about Victoria now to know that once she started something, she didn't stop until the job was done. The best thing he could do for her right now was to be supportive.

After Gina had gone, he went in to his wife.

"Poor girl," she said.

"What do you intend to do?" Because she would do something. He was sure of that.

She took a deep breath. "Well, first of all, I'm going to make sure that Gina has a lawyer and that Larry is held responsible for his child if he's proven to be the father. Then I'm going with Gina to pay a quiet visit to her parents. She says she wants to keep the baby. I'm hoping that if she does that, she'll get their support."

Caleb gave his wife a wry smile. "And you intend to see that that happens."

"I'm going to try, Caleb. Don't ask me not to try."

He shook his head. "I wasn't thinking of doing any such thing. I was only going to ask if you needed my help."

She gave him a grateful smile. "Not yet. I don't think so. Gina's father is a very private man. It will take him a while to get used to the truth. Until he does, it would be best to keep things low-key."

Caleb nodded. It was late. He supposed he really should get to work. He turned toward the door.

"Caleb?"

He looked over his shoulder.

"Thank you," she said, "for offering to help. You're—"

"I'm your husband," he said, knowing that she was going to spout off some nonsense about him being a noble kind of guy.

He wasn't noble, but he was beginning to think that his wife was. Gina had been so sure that Victoria was a person she could turn to. He wondered how many others she had quietly helped. His wife was turning out to be even more intriguing than he had thought at first.

"A delivery for you, Mrs. Fremont," William, the delivery boy for the florist, said, handing over a vase filled with red and white roses.

Victoria blinked. She took the flowers from William and peeked at the card.

To my wife, a noble lady during the day, a tigress at night.

Victoria's heart started to pound. Heat flooded her body.

"What's it say?" Lindsay Dufray asked.

Quickly Victoria stuffed the card in her pocket. "It says Happy Three-Week Anniversary," she lied.

"Hmm, I would have thought that a man with a body and a face and a reputation like Caleb's could come up with something more original than that," Lindsay said.

"It's a very nice sentiment, and Caleb is quite original," Victoria insisted.

Several women grinned.

"I didn't mean in bed," Victoria said.

Phillipa Parker raised one brow. "He's not original in bed?"

Oh no, this conversation was going downhill swiftly. "You all know very well what I meant," she said. "Caleb is…"

And suddenly she wondered just what Caleb was. For three weeks she had been married to him. He had made love to her, gently at times, fiercely at others. He knew how to make fire lick through her veins with just a look or the slightest touch. She craved him night and day, but what did she actually know about her husband?

"He's generous," she said, remembering his offer to help this morning.

"No one said he wasn't, hon. What's that paper stick-ing in among the flowers?" one woman asked.

Victoria looked, and sure enough there was another card folded in with the blooms. She slipped it out and put it in her pocket with the other card.

Jeanette Ollitson laughed. "I'll bet it's sizzling. I'll bet he's telling you what he wants to do with you in bed tonight," the woman said.

Victoria felt as if she were suffocating. "Are you going to buy that book or read it all right here in the store?" she asked in an uncharacteristically grumpy tone.

The other woman laughed. "I'm buying it, you goose. And don't get mad. I know it's no one's business but yours what that handsome husband of yours does with you after hours. He's been good for you, though, Victoria. Admit it. You look…softer."

Immediately Victoria felt contrite. "I didn't mean that comment about the book. It's just that I'm kind of—"

"Private, and a new bride to boot," someone else said. "Leave her alone, Jeanette."

"All right, sweetie. No more comments about your husband's prowess in bed. As if any of us here really know the truth about that, anyway. We just always liked to speculate. You're the only one who really knows him deep down and inside out, hon."

But she didn't, Victoria thought, later that day. She knew that he had been kind to her. She knew that he was an accomplished lover. She knew that he wrote riveting copy for the newspaper. And, she thought, gazing at the piece of paper she had fished from her pocket, she knew that he was a man who stood by his promises. The piece of paper contained the names, addresses and phone numbers of three attorneys in Dalloway. He had asked how he might help her and when she had told him that they had to keep things quiet, he had provided her with a means of doing that. She hadn't known any lawyers in Dalloway. She had the feeling that these men knew Caleb personally. He had given her a starting place to help Gina.

He was a good man. That was probably more than many wives could say of their husbands. What more did she really need to know, anyway?

"You've been a journalist for a long time, haven't you?"

Caleb looked up from the kitchen table into his wife's pretty eyes. "I suppose so. Why?"

"I was thinking—I've read most of what you've written these past few years, but…if you wouldn't mind, I'd like to see some of the things you wrote in your earlier days."

He grinned. "Ah, my wife…always interested in dry history."

"I can't imagine anything you ever wrote was dry."

"You're probably right. *Dry* was most likely the wrong word. I think the term *embarrassing drivel* might fit my earlier work pretty well."

Victoria frowned. Then she cocked her head and turned her frown into a devious smile. "I suppose that means you're too afraid to show it to me."

Caleb reached forward and brushed his thumb across his wife's nose. Then he rose and leaned across the table to drop a kiss on her lips as well. "A word of advice, my wife," he said as he sat back down. "You're not made for this game. I can't be dared into doing things."

She looked absolutely crestfallen and more than a little embarrassed.

"But I'm a sucker for women with brains," he said. "If you look in the black trunk that's in the basement, you'll probably find some of the stuff I wrote when I was fresh out of school and working for the *Dalloway Press*. Forgive me if I don't read over your shoulder. Some things are best put in a box and forgotten."

"They couldn't be that bad."

He gave her a look that said maybe her brain wasn't all that he had supposed it to be. "Victoria, why on earth do you want to read this stuff?"

She stirred her coffee and didn't look up. "It occurred to me today that we're still virtual strangers."

"That continues to bother you, doesn't it? The fact that I talked you into this."

She gazed directly into his eyes. "Most of the time I don't think of it," she admitted.

But there were other times, he knew, that she did. Why shouldn't she? He did the same. They shared a bed, they shared passion, they shared a common goal to get her pregnant and they also shared a goal of ending this marriage as soon as possible. Caleb felt an uncomfortable twinge, almost a deep pain. Well, why not? He and his wife had a most unconventional marriage. It wasn't unreasonable for her to feel regrets.

And he had absolutely no business thinking that he hoped it would take a good long time for her to conceive. It was a selfish thought born out of the fact that she was a fascinating woman. He wanted her. Too much, it seemed. No doubt it was a good thing that they had agreed to end everything as soon as conception was evident.

"If you really don't want me to read your early work, then I won't," she said, and he knew that she meant it. She was a woman of her word, a woman like no other he had ever met.

And unwise as it was, he rose and walked around the table. He stood behind her and slid his hands down over her shoulders. He leaned forward and kissed her neck.

She turned in her chair and he kissed her more fully.

"Read what you like, do as you like. Just come with me now," he whispered.

She did. And it was as wonderful as it had been the night before and the night before. With heat and passion like this, he couldn't keep his hands from her.

Surely she would conceive soon. And he would be forced to give her up.

"Stay," he said, when she raised up and stared down at him, her hair falling forward and brushing against his chest.

"I wasn't leaving," she promised. Then she smiled. "I've been told that women are crazy for your touch. I believe there's probably some truth in that. Touch me again," she said.

He smiled lazily. "I like a woman—"

"I know. With brains," she whispered.

"No. I like a woman like you," he said. "Right now my brain isn't functioning all that well. I'm hoping yours isn't either."

"I'm completely clueless." She kissed his chest. "I haven't a thought in the world beyond touching you."

But she would, he knew. She had a collection of pregnancy tests, and sometime tomorrow she would test herself.

There was a reason for this marriage. Making a baby. So they would make a baby.

Caleb took his wife into his arms and loved her and tried to give her a child. He wanted to please her. In every way.

Chapter Eleven

Caleb passed Gina Gregory on the street and couldn't help noticing that she was looking much calmer today. She was with her mother, and the two of them were chatting calmly. Obviously Victoria—or something—had made a difference in their lives.

When he got home after work, he asked her about it.

"What did you end up doing?"

"Not all that much. Larry agreed, after talking to the attorney, to pay child support, and I explained to Gina's parents what a help she's been with the store and that I would definitely help her out as much as I could and make sure she had time for the baby once it came. I directed them to some classes at the hospital for prospective new parents and grandparents. They talked about the possibilities of leaving the area, but Gina loves it here, she loves her work and I know that people here will support her. She's such a sweetheart. In the end, they agreed to stay and to help her as much as they could. I think they'll be good grandparents and champions of their daughter with a little time and effort."

He gazed at her incredulously. "So you didn't do much?"

"Not really."

"You, sweet wife, are very good at downplaying your contributions. I know Ray Gregory, and he isn't the kind of man who would come around easily."

She had the good grace to look a bit sheepish. "But in the end, he did," she said firmly. "That's all that matters."

"What did you have to promise him?"

"More hours for Gina. A turn at baby-sitting now and then. Threatening anyone who bad-mouthed his daughter in my store. And a stroller, high chair, crib and changing table. Not anything I wouldn't have volunteered to do, anyway."

He laughed and lifted her from her chair and swung her around. "And I'm sure you broached all this to him in just that quiet, matter-of-fact voice, didn't you? The man did not have a chance."

"Nonsense, I didn't do anything anyone else wouldn't have done."

But she had, Caleb knew. She had cared when others would have simply gossiped and pointed fingers. There were depths to her that he had never imagined. He wondered what more he would uncover about her if he looked.

But he wasn't sure he should look. Might be dangerous to grow to care too much about this lady, and he was afraid that he had already waded in too deep.

"And how about you?" she asked. "What were you doing, telling me that your earlier writing was garbage. It was wonderful, passionate stuff."

He frowned. "It was idealistic."

"You were young. You were supposed to be idealistic."

"I was never supposed to be idealistic. I never wanted to be."

She stopped shaking the paper and looked at him. "Why not?"

He didn't say anything.

"Caleb? Am I prying too deep?"

She seemed worried. He remembered his earlier thought that she cared about people. He didn't want her worrying about him.

"My news is old news, Victoria. My mother was a woman who worshipped my father, while he...well, let's just say that he barely noticed she existed most of the time. He had a full social life outside of his marriage. He made her miserable and she was prone to blaming herself. One day she was hit by a car. I could never get it out of my head that she was thinking about him and distracted when that happened. I've seen things like that happen to family and friends time and time again. People are inherently selfish, Victoria. There are no fairy tales, no real happily-ever-afters, and clinging to ideals is foolish. I'm surprised that I even wrote that stuff. I should probably have gotten rid of those years ago." He looked at the papers.

She clutched them more tightly. "Don't even think about disposing of these. It would be a disservice to the world of journalism. This is a piece of history," she insisted. "And they were very good articles. That's not an idealist talking, either. I run a bookstore. I know writing."

He shoved his hands in his pockets.

"Caleb?"

He looked at her.

"I'm sorry about your mother."

"Don't be. She married him. She most likely knew what he was when she took the step."

And if that wasn't putting it plainly, he didn't know what it was. Victoria had married him, and he was not a settling-down kind of guy. Any day now he would start feeling that old itching to move on that he always eventually felt with the women in his life. He was definitely not the kind of man a woman like Victoria should have. But for now, he was what she was stuck with.

Still, Caleb couldn't bring himself to make love with her that night. He had caught her looking at her pregnancy test this morning. The results had obviously been negative, and the look on her face would have broken any man's heart.

He didn't want her to go through that again tomorrow.

So this evening, he simply held her and he hoped that he was at least a little bit wrong about idealism. He had the feeling that Victoria, deep in her bones, was an idealist. For once, for just this once, he hoped dreams came true.

Victoria woke up feeling nervous and anxious and she couldn't understand why. Although…well, yes, she did actually know why she was feeling that way.

Caleb hadn't made love with her last night. He had merely held her the way he had on that first night they were married. She wondered if he was regretting his decision to enter into this marriage.

"Heck, he probably regretted it from the word go," she said to herself. "He only did it because he was worried about me, and now he's got me full-time. He's probably wondering how he got saddled with a crazy woman who solicited strangers to father her child."

"Crazy," Bob squawked. "Crazy woman. Hellfire."

"Thank you for adding to the conversation," she told the old bird.

She wondered if the *new* had worn off the marriage. Maybe Caleb was tired of making love to her. After all, in the past he could change partners as much as he pleased.

"Don't start feeling sorry for yourself," she whispered. "It's undignified."

And yet, not long afterward she found herself peeking in the door of the Renewal *Gazette*. She was not a coward and she might as well be straightforward and honest with her husband. She should let him know that he could get out of this marriage whenever he pleased. He had absolutely no obligation to her.

She found Denise beneath a sea of paperwork.

"You're looking for that handsome husband of yours, aren't you?" Denise asked. "I'll have to let him know you came by. He's not here."

"Oh, it wasn't important," Victoria said, feeling embarrassed and beginning to back out. "I hope I wasn't interrupting your work."

"Hey, hon, if it's between a husband and a wife, it's important. And don't ever worry about interrupting my work. I take every break Caleb will give me. At least he doesn't ask me to do those charity luncheons. That's where he is right now, addressing a group in Dalloway that provides scholarships for orphans. He does an awful lot of that stuff. Seems he's in demand as a speaker and the groups bring in more money when he comes. I'm not surprised you didn't know, though. He doesn't like anyone to know, and he's threatened to fire me if I squeak a word, but I figured you don't count. You're his wife."

"You're telling me Caleb gets paid to speak to charitable organizations."

Denise gave Victoria a honey-are-you-kidding look. "You know him better than that. They offer him money, but he donates every penny of it back. He says he does it because it's the civic duty of a journalist to contribute to society. I think he just likes helping people and he doesn't want anyone to think he's soft."

Victoria smiled. "I think you may be one of the most brilliant women I've met," she told Denise.

"Finally, recognition. Your husband thinks I'm a pain in the butt."

"My husband adores you, and rightly so," Victoria countered.

Denise practically glowed. "We won't let him know you told me that. Caleb and I operate best when we're fighting."

"Your secret is mine." And Victoria crossed her heart. She left the office smiling, but on the way back to her store, her brows creased in a frown. Caleb regularly contributed his time and his brilliant mind to good causes? Somehow that didn't surprise her. Neither did the fact that he kept his actions a secret.

Caleb was a giving man. He gave long hours to the newspaper, he gave to Renewal and to the surrounding communities. He believed in obligations and in taking care of those who needed care. No wonder he was in demand.

And who could blame such a man for wanting to keep the rest of his life to himself? He'd seen the dark side of love, the demanding and careless side. He'd decided he didn't want that for himself, and Victoria certainly couldn't blame him for that. She just wished she would hurry up and get pregnant so Caleb would feel free of any obligation to her.

Victoria was really an amazing woman if a man made the attempt to simply notice what very few people noticed, Caleb realized one day when he came home to find her crooning over a sickly little kitten. Not that he hadn't already realized that. It had surprised him the day he realized that he wasn't itching to run. In fact, he looked forward to coming home and just talking to her. Every single night. He loved making love with her. Victoria was a delight and a surprise every day. And now here she was, getting all gooey over the ugliest cat that had surely ever drawn breath.

"Friend of yours?" he asked.

"I don't think she belongs to anyone. At least not anymore," Victoria said. "No tags, no signs up about lost kittens. You haven't had anyone coming in today to run an ad, have you?"

"Afraid not." And he was genuinely sorry since his wife looked so sad.

"Someone must have wanted to get rid of her. Just threw her out like so much garbage," she said indignantly.

Caleb stilled. It was very similar to a statement his mother had made to his father, and one a woman had once made to him. He forced back the sick feeling.

"What will you do with her?"

"Fatten her up, I guess," Victoria said, and he was finally relieved to see a tracc of a smile in his wife's expressive eyes.

And that was exactly what she did. She nurtured that kitten, she fed it and cared for it and worried over it. She soothed Bob's jealous ruffled feathers, fussing over him as well, and she worked at her forlorn little family. Then one day when the kitten was almost well, Alice Myers and her seven-year-old daughter, Nolie, were walking by the house while Caleb and Victoria were in the yard.

"Ohh." Nolie's eyes lit up as she watched the kitten tumbling on the ground trying to catch a butterfly. "Can I touch?" she asked Victoria.

Caleb watched as Nolie's eyes lit up. He could see the second his wife's heart melted. "She loves to be rubbed," Victoria confessed.

"What's her name?"

"Um, I'm not sure. She's pretty new around here. What do you think would be a good name?"

Nolie thought. She cocked her head to one side. "Butterfly," she said. "I like Butterfly." And she knelt down and played with the little kitten until her mother finally tugged on her hand.

"Come on, pumpkin," Alice told her child. "We have to let Mr. and Mrs. Fremont get back to their business. I'm afraid Nolie's a little overexcited," she explained. "Our own cat was old and she finally passed away. I couldn't bring myself to get another."

She urged her daughter to go, but as they left, Nolie's eyes kept returning to the kitten. Her mother looked distressed. "It probably wasn't a good idea to stop by," she said.

"Stop by anytime," Victoria said. "Please." Caleb noticed that her own eyes were sad as she looked at the little girl.

Two days later, he came home to find Victoria in the kitchen with Bob.

"No little bundle of fluff about today?" he asked. "Did she finally decide to go down for a nap?"

Victoria gave a slight shrug. Then she looked up at Caleb with guilty eyes. "I gave her to Nolie. I'm sure I should have checked with you first."

Caleb couldn't help smiling. "She was your kitten, Victoria," he said, taking his wife's hands, "and I know you were getting attached to her. You just couldn't help yourself, though, could you?"

"A child should have a pet," she said firmly.

"Ah, I see." He crossed his arms and settled his hips against the counter. "So what kind of pet did you have?"

Victoria went back to chopping vegetables for dinner.

"Umm, tough question, I see," he coaxed.

She stopped. She gave him that imperious look that he had learned to love. "I didn't have a pet at all. My parents were theater people. Pets weren't practical, at least not pets that ran around on four legs. Bob didn't come along until later, and even then, he wasn't considered a pet. He became a part of the act. I wasn't supposed to touch."

But a child should have a pet, she'd said. Caleb felt his heart clench at the thought of a much younger Victoria longing for a kitten to cuddle.

"You were an only child?"

She shrugged. "Not that uncommon."

No, he was an only child himself, but he could tell by her expression that their experiences had been different. For all of his parents' differences, they had, for the most part, catered to his deepest needs.

"So your parents were theater people," he said. "That must have been exciting."

She gave him a small smile and shook her head. "You're wondering how a bland woman like myself fit into the theater."

"I would never describe you as bland."

"I would."

"Then you need a new dictionary." He crossed his arms.

She delighted him by smiling. "Caleb, I was a disaster. My parents longed to have a daughter who would run out on the stage full tilt, throw herself into character and completely charm the audience. I think they sometimes thought that the stork really did bring me and that I was delivered to the wrong couple. Don't get me wrong. They loved me in their way. They were just completely bewildered by me. I wasn't anything like what they had expected when they conceived. It took us a long time to reach a consensus. They did all the stage stuff. I only worked behind the scenes."

He'd just bet that she worked very hard, too. Her parents were lucky to have had her. But if he said that, she would only deny it.

"Well, it looks like Bob eventually evolved into a pet," he said.

Victoria's smile grew wide. "I don't think Bob was any more suited to the stage than I was. He kept saying the wrong things at the wrong time. We're a pair, aren't we, old guy?"

Bob pretended he didn't understand. He didn't say a word.

"So what do you say, Bob?" Caleb asked. "Should we add a new member to our family? A kitten or a puppy? Maybe even a lady friend for you?"

Bob still didn't talk, but he looked somewhat interested.

But Victoria shook her head. "We can't do that, Caleb. We're not a family, and once the baby is conceived, all this will end. It wouldn't be a good idea to start bringing in new members and forming ties. I probably shouldn't have taken in the kitten. It was best to give her to Nolie."

Her voice was firm, but she couldn't hide the wistful look in her eyes. Caleb wanted to hit something, but he knew that she was right. Pretending they were a real family would only complicate the situation.

But darn it, when this was over, he was giving her a pet. He wanted her to have that much at least. Hell, he wanted her to have everything.

More than that, he just wanted her. And he was starting to want her more and more with each day. That was just too bad, because she didn't want anything of him except what he could contribute toward making a baby, and he would be wise to remember that. Her parents had tried to force her to do things she didn't want to do and to be something she didn't want to be and to feel things she couldn't feel. He was never going to treat her that way.

Victoria was making coffee the next morning when the telephone rang. She picked it up and said hello.

For several seconds there was silence on the line. "I'm sorry, I think I have the wrong number," a feminine voice finally said. "I was trying to reach Caleb Fremont."

Victoria felt a jolt. The voice was low and seductive.

"Not at all," she said into the receiver. "Let me put him on the line." And she handed the phone to Caleb.

He spoke into the receiver, then listened, a frown denting his forehead.

"No, I'm afraid that won't be possible," he said, and then listened some more.

"Yes, Victoria is my wife," he continued. "We've only been married a short time. It was…a whirlwind courtship one might say."

Victoria felt panic begin to climb inside her as Caleb finished his conversation and hung up the telephone. She meant to keep her mouth shut.

"An old girlfriend?" she asked, in spite of her good intentions.

"A friend," Caleb corrected her. "Nothing serious."

But of course Caleb never had serious relationships. Serious wasn't what he wanted. He liked sweet and hot and fast, according to the neighborhood gossip that had circulated prior to her marriage. It occurred to Victoria that all gossip had ceased since she had married him. At least all gossip had ceased that was uttered in her presence. She would just bet that people still talked. She wondered what the local gossips would think of this phone call.

But she knew what they would say. Caleb Fremont was still in demand. Women still wanted him, but he was no longer free. Pain and guilt sluiced through her.

"That was nice of her to call," she managed to say.

Caleb gave her a look. "When I'm married, Victoria," he said, carefully, his voice deep and strong. "I'm very married."

She nodded, but inside she was thinking that he shouldn't be married. He'd only married her to help her. If he had been single, he and that woman with the beautiful voice would be making arrangements to…to do what she and Caleb did every night. Her heart tightened until she could barely breathe.

It had been three months since she and Caleb had married. She still hadn't conceived in spite of all their efforts. She knew that three months wasn't that long, and yet she also knew that she had to free Caleb soon.

Caleb was gathering his things for the walk into town. His days usually began earlier than hers.

"Caleb," she said, touching his sleeve.

He looked down at her and her resolve faltered. She forced away her reservations.

"I—I… Do you think you could be home early?" she asked.

"If you need me to," he said. "Is something wrong?"

She shook her head vehemently. "No. No. Not at all. I just want to— I thought we might—" She looked away.

"Victoria?"

"I think the time is right," she whispered.

And suddenly her husband's hands were at her waist. She swayed toward him, but she couldn't hide her embarrassment at having asked.

"Victoria," he murmured against her ear. "I meant what I said. I'm very married. You're my wife. When you want something, ask. When you need something, tell me. And if you think I'm going to find it a chore to make love with you, you couldn't be more wrong."

He placed his thumb beneath her chin and nudged her head up. He stared directly into her eyes. "I'll be home very early today," he told her. "Be ready." And he kissed her, so deeply that her head swam and her knees nearly buckled.

As Caleb went out the door, she touched her lips. She definitely needed to free Caleb soon. For her own sake.

Perhaps she would just pay a call to the doctor…

Chapter Twelve

"Well, you're certainly looking rested and hearty," Denise told Caleb when he walked in the door of the newspaper several weeks later. "A person might almost think that marriage agrees with you."

"Fishing, Denise?"

"Always."

"Well then, for your information, marriage is agreeing with me very well."

It was the answer he was expected to give, but as Caleb moved into his office, he realized that he hadn't been lying. Living with Victoria and having her in his arms every night was a delight. "Let's teach Bob some new words," he had teased just the other day, and she had gotten that delightfully prim look about her.

"What kind of words?" she had asked.

"Um, I don't know. 'Hello' or 'You're great, Caleb,' might be nice."

She had smiled. "Oh, you mean boring words. I thought you meant something spicy."

He laughed. "You would object to that?"

She had shrugged. "Bob already knows all those words. He was a stage bird. Bob taught *me* how to swear." Then she had chuckled. "You can't imagine how shocked my mother was when I let loose with a stream of…um, colorful invectives and then explained that I had gotten all of them from our bird."

"Really?" he had asked her with a grin. "Whisper something dirty to me."

And to his surprise, she had leaned forward, cupped her delicate hand around his ear and uttered a word that she never would have used under ordinary circumstances. "Bob used to belong to a military man," she explained. "And if you ever tell anyone what I said, I will…I will…"

"You'll what?" he had asked as he took his pretty wife in his arms and dipped her back to steal a kiss. Her lips were delicious. All of her was delicious.

"I'll make you read yesterday's book of the day," she finally said as she gazed up at him with eyes that made him want to kiss her again.

"What was it?" he asked.

"Exotic Dancing for Men," she told him.

Caleb laughed. "Let's dance, then," he said. And they did.

* * *

"Caleb? Caleb? Are you here in the room with me or are you on some desert island with a gorgeous woman?" Denise demanded.

"What?" he asked. He wondered if she knew how close she was to the truth. Probably. Denise didn't miss much.

"Are we working today?"

He nodded. "Later?"

Denise's eyes widened. "Later? Later? Hello, did aliens steal my boss? Are you really Caleb Fremont?"

He smiled, but not much. There was something bothering him, something he needed to know the answer to. An observant woman like Denise was probably his best bet.

"Denise, have you noticed anything different about my wife lately?"

"Besides the fact that she's been wearing the same expression you have been? The one that makes her look as if an asteroid could drop on the roof of her bookstore and she wouldn't notice?"

"That's not what I meant." And he wasn't sure he believed Denise, anyway. He and Victoria had been constantly in each other's company lately. They had made long, languorous love night after night, sometimes frantically, but then that was part of Victoria's bargain. He knew she enjoyed it, he gave her pleasure, but her chief aim had always been to have a baby. He tried to forget that part when she was in his arms.

Denise shrugged. "All right, there are moments—not often—when she looks a little stressed, maybe worried.

Junie Martin said that she asked for a copy of *What to Do When You're Expecting* the other day, and Victoria looked as if she wanted to cry. We just all assumed that it was that time of the month."

Caleb frowned. "My wife does not get emotional at that time of the month."

Denise shrugged. "Sorry, it was just a guess, but it's not like Victoria to show emotion in public at all. Not that she did then. Junie said that two seconds later, Victoria was smiling and being as professional as ever."

Oh, yes, that was his Victoria. She hid her concerns. She didn't share them with anyone. For some reason that put him into a black mood. He wanted to shake the walls, to shake Victoria and ask her what was bothering her. But he knew she wouldn't say.

Because she didn't really consider him to be her husband. Their marriage wasn't real.

He slammed his hand down on his desk and uttered a word he hadn't uttered in years. Bob would have been proud.

"Oh, yeah, that'll make her open up," Denise remarked.

Caleb blew out a sigh. "Sorry," he said, as he sat down and prepared for work. Denise was right. If he wanted his wife to share her thoughts with him, he was going to have to set the stage and coax her secrets from her.

Victoria felt as if someone had just dropped a heavy weight on her head. Or maybe as if something more basic had happened. She had come up against the simple truth, and the truth was unpleasant.

Slowly she walked down the street toward home,

trying very hard to appear normal. Against her most basic instincts, she didn't cover her mouth with her hands or allow her tears to well up. Of course, the pain in her heart could not be stopped.

For weeks now she had felt as if she had somehow tricked Caleb, or at least misled him, however unintentionally. As early as this morning, she had moved into his arms, eager to be close to him.

"Touch me, please," she had said.

"What a wonderful way to wake up," he had told her, and then he had taken her close to his heart and made her feel things she had never envisioned a few months ago. And her reactions had not just been physical, either. If that were the case, this pain would not be so cutting, the truth so bitter.

"I have to end it," she told herself as she walked on. "I have to be honest."

But her feet felt sluggish. The air was like heavy syrup she was trudging through. She would go home, she would make dinner and then she would tell him everything.

"No, not everything," she said. She couldn't tell him everything. If she did, then she would have to admit the truth to herself, and even now, she couldn't bring herself to face the truth.

"Hello, Mrs. Fremont," Misty said as Victoria passed her on the street. "My baby is having a birthday party today. Can you come?"

Suddenly, without warning, quick tears filled Victoria's eyes. "I'm sorry, sweetie, I can't be there this time, but wish her happy birthday for me, all right?"

"'Kay," Misty said. "It's all right, Mrs. Fremont. You

don't have to cry. My baby understands. My mommy tells me that sometimes things happen."

"Your mommy is very smart," Victoria agreed, with a watery smile. "Thank you, Misty."

Victoria walked on home and moved toward the kitchen, realizing that this room, this house, this whole life wouldn't be hers much longer. She was here playing make-believe, just like Misty.

But for one more day, she could pretend that things were normal with her and Caleb. For today, she could still be his wife. She could still love him.

That one little thought almost tripped her up, and she stumbled slightly. But she didn't deny the truth. She didn't even question it. After all, didn't all women love him? And wasn't she the one woman who had been blessed to spend the last few months alone with him? Why should she be surprised that the inevitable had happened?

She wasn't surprised. She was just desolate, and she was determined to hide her feelings from him. They had started this as a partnership, they had entered into this marriage for a purely practical reason and now that reason was gone. End of story. She would buck up and do the right thing.

He would never know the truth.

Victoria pushed open the door of the kitchen, prepared to end her marriage as it had begun. Quietly.

She was barely into the room when strong arms enveloped her. Caleb dropped a kiss on the side of her neck. He swept her up into an embrace.

"Welcome home, Mrs. Fremont," he said, with a delicious look in his eyes.

Victoria blinked. She did her best not to react to Caleb's nearness. She failed miserably.

Courage, she told herself. *Act normally. Don't let him know you're hurting.*

She smiled up at her husband. "What's this? Did Denise kick you out of the office?"

He laughed. "Ah, you've found me out. She's been wanting to do that for years. Finally she staged a mutiny. Looks like you're stuck with me tonight. Well, with me and Bob. And Lionel."

Victoria raised her brows. "Lionel?"

"Um, I didn't tell you about Lionel?"

"Is he a newspaperman?"

Caleb laughed. "Could be. I did put him down on some newspaper and he sniffed around as if he might be interested someday."

"You want to explain that, my husband?" She had to say it. It felt so good, so right on her tongue. She wanted to keep standing in the circle of Caleb's arms forever, to keep looking up into his eyes until eternities passed away. Even if she was leaving tomorrow.

Caleb lifted one shoulder and gave her a sheepish look. "Well…when Denise demanded that I get my butt out of the office…"

"She did not."

"Okay, she didn't. I just left."

"I'm guessing you had a good reason."

"Oh, absolutely." He bent and nuzzled her neck again. She trembled and wanted to ask him to do that again, but she managed to hold back.

"You want to share that reason?"

"Oh, yeah, I do. I had something important to do."

"And that was…" she prompted.

"I had to pick up Lionel, even though I didn't know it at the time. I only knew that I had to swing by the shelter. Once I got there, it was clear that Lionel had everyone up in arms and he was in danger of being thrown out into the cold."

"Hmm," she said, leaning back in her husband's arms. "It's summer."

"Yes, but it can be a cold world if you're on your own."

She knew that. She knew it so well. She waited, but when Caleb kissed her lips and didn't show any signs of taking the conversation further, she kissed him back, then took her lips half a breath away.

"Caleb, tell me why you're home. Don't sugarcoat it, either."

"All right, Victoria. I'm home because we've been married four months, or we will have been soon. I wanted to give you a gift."

"Oh." She couldn't keep the distress from her voice. "I don't have anything for you."

"That's all right. I'll take a kiss or two." And he took them. "Now, hold out your hands."

She did, and Caleb reached into his pocket. He placed a little puppy into her grasp.

"Lionel?" she guessed.

"Yes, I guess he does look a bit like a lion. A puny one with hair that sticks up in all the wrong directions. He's a little rambunctious and he likes to chew on things and I'm pretty sure he believes he's the real item straight from Africa, because he's been threatening all the other puppies at the shelter. We're going to have to teach him some manners. Maybe we can get Bob to take him in hand."

She looked down at the little growling ball of fluff, and hot tears filled her eyes.

"You said that every child should have a pet. You told me you didn't have one. I know you're not a child, sweetheart, and I would never try to replace Bob, but I just thought… Well, I'm sure that someone else will adopt him if we take him back."

He started to take Lionel from her hands. She was pretty sure the scruffy puppy was going back in her husband's pocket. She was also pretty sure that the cute little creature had scratched holes in her husband's expensive suit.

"He's perfect," she said, holding on. "Thank you." The tears began to fall.

"Victoria," Caleb said, his voice thick. "I'm sorry. You've been sad at times lately. I've noticed. I only wanted to make you happy."

"You have," she said, though her voice was thick.

"I can see that." He thumbed away one fat tear that was coursing down her cheek.

She shook her head and with a supreme effort, willed the tears to stop. "I have been happy, Caleb. And I really appreciate everything you've done for me, including Lionel, but…"

"Ah, there's always a but, isn't there. What's wrong, Mrs. Fremont?"

She gazed at him and hoped he couldn't read her mind or what was in her eyes or heart.

Victoria shook her head. "I'm afraid I can't be Mrs. Fremont any longer."

Caleb seemed to freeze. His eyes grew fierce. He stared at her with a gaze like red lasers. "I'm assuming you're going to explain that statement."

"Yes. Yes, I am. I've been to see the doctor. Several times lately. I…I can't tell you why I went. I just…suspected something was wrong."

He took the puppy from her and placed him back in his pocket. He wrapped his arms around her tightly. "What's wrong?" His voice was rough, heavy, harsh, the sound like nothing she had ever heard from her light-hearted husband.

She braced her hands on his chest. "Nothing fatal. Nothing terrible, I assure you. I just…there's no reason for us to be married anymore is all. I can't have children. The possibility just doesn't exist. I can show you the test results, the paperwork, the literature that pertains to my condition, but the end result will still be the same. I'm not going to have children, Caleb. There was no reason for us to marry. I'm going back home tomorrow. I'll call my lawyer and start the process."

He didn't say a word.

"I'm sorry I let you marry me," she told him. "I always knew it was a mistake, but I was selfish." In so many ways, she thought. She hadn't been truthful with herself or with him when they had gotten married. "But now it's over. I…I hope we can go on being friends. I'll always be grateful to you."

"You'll be grateful." He said the words as if she had

insulted him. His expression was dark, his hands like bands of steel. He looked away—he loosened his grip.

"Hell, Victoria." He blew out a breath. "I'm so damn sorry about the baby. I know how much this meant to you."

"It's okay."

"It's not okay. It's damned unfair."

It was, and she knew when the truth finally registered and she realized that she would spend the rest of her life alone, she would hurt for the loss of the child she had wanted so badly. But right now, the truth hadn't registered. Her inability to have a baby hardly even seemed to matter, except for one thing. It meant that she and Caleb were over, and that pain was almost too much to bear.

She loved him, and she had to give him up. Now, before he noticed the truth, before he discovered that she was just like every other woman in Renewal. She was his for the taking, even if he didn't want her.

"Goodbye, Caleb," she told him. "Thank you. For everything."

He took a step toward her. "You don't have to go yet. You could stay the night."

She could, but there was no reason for them to touch anymore, and if she stayed in this house and slept apart from him…the night would be far too long and dark.

Victoria searched for some way to run without revealing her heart. "It's probably best if Lionel begins his first night away from the shelter in the place that he will finally call home."

The excuse sounded lame to her own ears.

Caleb studied her for a second. Then he nodded curtly. "I'll help you pack. I'll take you home."

It didn't take long. When they were standing on her doorstep, the door open behind her, with Bob and Lionel safely ensconced inside, she looked up at Caleb, unsure what to do. Finally she held out her hand.

"You've been…a good friend, Caleb," she said.

He took her hand. And then he placed it around his neck. He slipped his hand to her waist and drew her close against him. He angled his mouth over hers and kissed her, his lips moving slowly over hers.

"I've been more, Victoria," he told her when he drew away. "And don't you ever forget it." Then he was gone, back to his world.

She almost stumbled toward him as he walked away, but with a supreme effort, she managed to hold herself still.

Behind her, she could hear the puppy scrambling around and Bob squawking.

She slipped into her house and shut the door. *Caleb,* she wanted to call out. *Don't let me do this. Let's go back to yesterday or three months ago and start over again. Please stay.* Instead she closed her eyes and let the tears fall.

"Hellfire," she finally said. The word didn't make her feel any better. Her thoughts were down the street with the man she loved, and she could not help wondering if he would be resuming his trips to Dalloway soon.

Chapter Thirteen

"People are talking about you." Denise said the words as if Caleb didn't know what she was talking about. He knew. He just didn't care.

"We have work to do, Denise," he reminded her.

"I know, but doesn't it bother you the least little bit that people are whispering behind your back?"

"People have always whispered behind my back."

"Yes, but now some of them are making a point of not buying the newspaper. Doesn't that bother you, even a little?"

It didn't. At least not yet. If things got so bad that the newspaper had to cut employees or if he had to shut down and lose his work, the only thing that gave him an outlet for his energy these days, then he might care.

"Leave it, Denise," he said.

"But they think that—"

"I know what they think. They're right. I should never have married Victoria."

Denise's mouth was hanging open. "Why—why—"

"Exactly," he said. No one knew why he and Victoria had married. No one knew why the marriage had ended. The obvious conclusion, that he had used Victoria for his own selfish physical needs, was the one everyone had jumped to.

And they were right.

He *had* used her, because while he had married her for what had seemed like a good reason, in the end he had been forced to admit that his reasons had been suspect. Victoria Holbrook had become a fever in his blood. He had wanted her, he had proposed marriage to her, he had taken her.

No matter how he had lied to himself and to her, there had been nothing logical about his reasons. It had all been pure emotion, the thing he had loathed and run from all his life.

Now he was paying the price. He knew the agony of those who love without any hope of reward.

He was an idiot, a jerk and a conniver. He had taken Victoria and now he had lost her. Let the people talk.

It didn't matter. Nothing mattered except how long it would take him to stop loving her.

He hoped it happened soon. Until then there was only work, and work was no substitute for Victoria in his arms.

"Are you sure? Can't you make it up with her somehow?"

"Denise." He practically roared his assistant's name.

She looked up, temporarily silenced.

"Dammit, I'm leaving," he told her.

"Where are you going?"

To hell, most likely. "To Dalloway."

She gasped. "Maybe everyone is right about you," she said, and he knew what she was thinking. Like everyone, she thought Dalloway's appeal for him was its women. Who cared? Dalloway was most likely where Victoria's doctor had been located, and he needed to talk to the man. Professional confidentiality or not, surely he could find out why Victoria couldn't have a child. Surely there was something that could be done. If he could just do this one thing for her...

"Forget it, Fremont," he muttered to himself. "Do it just for her or not at all. She isn't going to love you, but you can at least try to help her."

And if he could, he would.

"There he goes," Jeanette Ollitson said with a sneer. "Still walking around this town like a king. Probably on his way to Dalloway right now."

Victoria felt as if she was going to be sick. She didn't say a word.

"Hon, don't you worry," Jeanette said. "People are on your side."

"What do you mean?"

"Hon, we all know what kind of a man he is. He did you wrong, and people in this town don't like that kind of thing. I don't buy that newspaper anymore. It's an inconvenience, but a person has to stand by their principles."

"Are you trying to tell me that Caleb is being punished because people think that he dumped me for a…a…"

"A hedonistic lifestyle." Jeanette supplied the words.

"But that's not true. Caleb didn't dump me. I dumped him."

"Of course you did." The woman patted Victoria's arm like a mother hen who was humoring her chick. "Just rest assured, Victoria, that we take care of our friends, and we don't let things like this go unpunished."

And with that the woman took her book and left.

"Jeanette, wait," Victoria said. But the woman just turned and waved.

Victoria looked across the room at Lindsay Dufray. "You don't think Caleb hurt me, do you?" she asked.

"Of course not, dear," Lindsay said, but it was clear to Victoria that her friend was just being nice.

Did everyone in town think that Caleb was a lowlife? Surely not, but it seemed that a fair amount did, and that was her fault. She hadn't told anyone that Caleb had married her to help her. To the people of Renewal, it had been a real marriage and one where she had ended up the loser.

"Well, you did lose," she told herself at the end of the day. She had fallen in love with Caleb and lost him, but that had been her fault, not his.

But now he was the one being made to pay the price. People were talking about him. Some were even turning their backs on him, hitting him in the one place where they could hurt him, his newspaper, his passion.

"Well, that is about to stop," she told herself firmly.

Her pride could be damned, but she was not going to let this go on for even one day longer.

"You want me to what?"

"You heard me, Denise," Victoria said. "He's not here, is he?"

"No, he left hours ago, and I have to tell you that that in itself was strange. He's been working like a madman ever since you two broke up."

Victoria faltered at that, but she refused to let herself think about what Caleb had been doing for the past week. Whatever he had been doing, he had been doing it without her. His life had gone on. It was the way things should be, and she had to learn to deal with that. Somehow she had to learn to submerge and stamp out what she felt for the man. If she didn't, she would never be able to stay in Renewal.

"He loves this newspaper," Victoria said, "and rightfully so. He built it, he made it what it is, and just as this letter says, Denise, he did not do a thing to deserve the wrath of the town. All Caleb did was try to help me. He wanted me to have the child I wanted, and he wanted to give that child a name. It was a good thing."

"Caleb was going to be a daddy?"

Victoria shook her head. "No, not exactly. Just…just read the letter, Denise, and print it. You can do that without running it past Caleb, can't you?"

The woman gave her a suspicious look. "Why don't you want him to know?"

"Because he would never run anything in the newspaper that was in his own self-interest. He would never use the *Gazette* for personal gain, but I was married to him. I don't have those qualms, and I don't like what people are saying about him or the fact that they're trying to hurt him through his newspaper."

Denise hesitated. "Are you in love with Caleb?"

Victoria didn't answer.

"Victoria?"

"That would be pretty foolish, wouldn't it?" Victoria asked.

"Probably, but—" Denise blew out a breath. "Who can blame you? Caleb hits women that way. And for the record, he has depths most people don't see," she said, as if telling Victoria something she didn't already know.

"Yes, he does. So you'll do as I ask?"

Denise considered it. "Might get me in trouble."

Victoria sighed.

"Wouldn't be the first time I was in trouble with the boss, though," Denise continued. "And I don't like people criticizing Caleb, especially if he was only trying to help you."

"That was all he was doing," Victoria said. "Thank you, Denise. I'll take full responsibility for this one." She handed over the piece of paper.

Caleb sat down at the table with his morning cup of coffee and the *Gazette*. He felt a twinge of guilt that Denise had been left with so much work yesterday, especially since he hadn't been able to talk Victoria's doctor into revealing a thing.

He would apologize to Denise when he got into the

office this morning, he thought, but then his gaze fell upon the letters page:

"To my friends in Renewal," the letter read.

Many of you know that Caleb Fremont and I married not long ago and that we're no longer together. What you probably don't know is that Caleb married me because I wanted a child and I was willing to go to desperate lengths to get one. I even went so far as to solicit total strangers in a personals ad.

But Caleb saved me from myself. He married me to protect me, to help me in my quest to have a child. He gave me the protection of his name. Unfortunately, nature had a different idea and so I have decided to end the marriage. I know there are those who think that Caleb hurt me somehow and I just have to say that nothing could be further from the truth. Caleb didn't hurt me. He gave me the greatest and most generous gift I have ever been given, and I will always be grateful. So I'm doing now what I should have done a long time ago. I'm telling the world and Renewal about the amazing thing Caleb did for me. I want everyone to know what a good man he is. You won't ever find a better one anywhere.

Caleb's cup was stalled somewhere between his newspaper and the table. His heart was threatening to stop beating. A large lump had lodged in his throat.

Victoria's name was at the bottom of the letter. For

a second he wondered if Denise had put her up to this, but then he remembered his pretty, prim and determined little wife. No one told Victoria what to do. She was unique among women.

He loved her desperately, but he wished she hadn't done this. Everyone knew the newspaper belonged to him. People might think that he had made her write the letter. They would think she was under his thumb. Victoria would hate that, and it just wasn't true. What should he do?

And for the first time that week, Caleb smiled just a bit. He pulled out his laptop.

Caleb was sitting at his desk at the *Gazette* early the next morning when he heard a commotion outside. He looked up just in time to see Victoria at the head of a mob headed his way. She was holding a newspaper with the pages folded back in her hand. He knew exactly what page it was opened to.

"Dear Friends and Neighbors," the letter said.

I want to tell you about a woman I know. For a brief while she was my wife. She's lived in Renewal now for a couple of years, yet many of us don't really know her, and that's a shame, because a woman like Victoria Holbrook doesn't come along very often. She's strong and intelligent, a woman who wanted a child and did all the right things to become a mother.

I'm sure those of you who know Victoria will agree that she would have been a wonderful mother, too, because she's good and kind and giving. In case you haven't noticed, she's given to all of us in this town in her own quiet way. She's brought a love of literature to Renewal, she gave us a comfortable place to read, she helps her neighbors when they're in trouble, she raises a kitten she loves and then turns it over to a child who needs it. Yet she's never asked for recognition, she never wanted any, and it's well past time we recognized her for the unique and wonderful woman she is.

You may have read her letter that explained our reasons for marrying. Well, I'm here to tell you that I was lucky to have had the opportunity to be Victoria's husband. In the future, I hope that more of you will stop by and get to know her better. As for myself, I love her and I always will.

It was signed Caleb Fremont, and it had been a terrible breach of his position to print the letter. He had hesitated over his last admission, because he didn't want to embarrass Victoria, but in the end, he had left it in, and he didn't regret a word.

Now he watched Victoria as she moved toward him, her head held high. She entered the open door of the *Gazette,* her entourage behind her, though she didn't seem to notice them.

Her eyes were troubled. She held out her newspaper. "Why did you write this?" she asked.

"You set yourself up with that letter the other day. You left yourself open for criticism. There are those who might condemn a woman who would marry a man with the sole aim of conceiving. I wanted the world to know you as you are."

She gazed at him with those lovely big brown eyes. "But what you said…at the end…"

He frowned. "I suppose some women might be insulted by that last. I've enjoyed a certain reputation. Are you insulted?" Caleb asked.

She took a step closer. "I'm confused. I don't understand."

He stepped around the desk. "What don't you understand, Victoria?"

The crowd shuffled back to give him greater access to her. She gazed up at him with troubled eyes. "You said…you said you loved me. Is it the truth?"

"Have you ever known me to print a lie?"

Slowly she shook her head. "No, you're not a liar. Your dedication to the truth is one of your greatest assets, but…"

"But what?"

She looked to the side. "But you never told me that you loved me before." Her voice was barely a whisper. "Perhaps we're not talking about the same thing when we use the word *love*. I hope we are."

The ache in his heart deepened. He knew she meant that she just wanted to be a loving friend. He should let her go, but she was here with him, and he longed to keep her here longer.

Caleb stepped closer. With just the tip of his index finger, he traced a line down her cheek. "You don't understand what I mean by love, Victoria? Maybe that's because you didn't come looking for love when you came to me. You wanted a baby."

He stroked her cheek and she trembled beneath his touch. When she raised her face to him, he saw a trace of tears in her beautiful eyes. "I think that maybe I lied to myself and to you about that," she whispered. "I think I came to you because I wanted you, and you were unattainable. You didn't date women from Renewal, and even if you had, I wouldn't be a woman you would choose. I guess I did want you all along."

Caleb's head was reeling. The world was spinning beneath his feet, and Victoria was looking stricken. He wanted to save her somehow.

"You wanted a baby," he corrected her.

She took a deep breath, and she looked up at him with great conviction in her eyes. "Yes," she agreed, "but mostly I wanted you."

He stopped breathing. She had said she wanted him, but women had wanted him before. He wanted more from Victoria. He wanted forever. She hadn't said that she loved him, too. He knew from experience that desire didn't equal love and that love didn't always flow both ways.

A hushed murmur had started at Victoria's revelation. It grew louder now, and as if she had just wakened from a trance, Victoria turned to look at the shocked faces of the people of the town. She gave Caleb one sudden stricken look.

Then she ran out of the building. Victoria never ran. Something was terribly wrong.

"Victoria!" Caleb called, and he started after her, but a sea of people rushed forward.

"What's going on here, Caleb?" someone asked. "That letter from Victoria was strange enough, but the one from you…is this all just a publicity stunt for the newspaper? Is it true that the *Gazette* is in big trouble?"

Caleb didn't answer. He didn't give a damn about the *Gazette*. Instead he pushed forward.

"Was the marriage really a sham?" someone else asked, blocking his way.

In the distance, he saw Victoria go around the corner. No, the marriage had not been a sham. It had been the most real thing in his life, Caleb realized.

"Excuse me. I have to find my wife," he said, pushing past the crowd as he ran out into the street after the woman he loved. He had to find out why she had run, and he had to make it right.

He went to the bookstore, but she wasn't there. He stopped at her house, but she wasn't there, either. He even tried his house, but came up empty-handed.

Finally, he knew it was useless. Victoria was in hiding, from herself or from him, he didn't know. But he knew one thing. He had found a woman worth loving and worth waiting for, and he would wait forever if he had to.

Caleb sat down on her steps and made himself comfortable.

It was dark by the time Victoria finally stopped walking and wandered home. She wondered if people had stopped laughing by now. Not that she cared. Only one person's opinion counted right now, and she didn't want to see him. Caleb had told her he loved her, but she knew now that what he meant by love and what she meant were two different things. She had said she wanted him, and he hadn't looked happy. He hadn't tried to stop her when she left him the day she ended the marriage. In fact, he hadn't said a word. In the weeks they had been separated, he hadn't asked her to come back, and he had only written the letter in the newspaper after she had forced his hand. As always, Caleb had done the gentlemanly thing, but it hadn't really meant a thing.

Slowly she moved up the stairs to the porch.

Hands reached out and caught at her. She squealed.

"Don't," Caleb's voice whispered. "Please don't run from me again, Victoria. Stay this time."

She stilled. She stayed.

He cupped her face in his hands. "I've had plenty of time to think while you've been gone," he said. "I realize that when you said you wanted me, you meant that you wanted me for the short-term. I also know that I probably embarrassed you when I announced that I loved you in a public newspaper. You've always been a private person. You've never liked the stage. I didn't mean to humiliate you or reveal your secrets, you know," he whispered. "Forgive me."

She leaned against him. She longed to stay there. "I'm the one who embarrassed myself. Now everyone knows that Victoria Holbrook asked Caleb Fremont, the most eligible bachelor in town, to love her."

His hands tightened on her. "Oh, but I *do* love you," he finally said. He bent and kissed her. She dared to hope.

"You've loved a lot of women," she answered, her voice cracking. "That woman who called you. I didn't want to be like her or all the others. I didn't want to be another one of those women who threw herself at you."

Her voice broke, and suddenly Caleb was kneeling before her. "Throw yourself at me," he whispered.

"What?"

"Throw yourself at me, Victoria. Please. Remember how you were going to seduce me once? Do it again."

Suddenly she wondered what Caleb was trying to do. "I don't appreciate being made fun of, Caleb."

"I would never make fun of the woman I love. I promise you that, love."

She bit her lip. "I know you just told me you loved me so I could save face with the people of the town after I publicly confessed that I threw myself at you and tried to bribe you. You didn't really mean that you loved me."

He took her hand and kissed her palm. She could feel him smiling against her skin. "I wonder if that means that you'll never ever try to seduce me again, Victoria, my love."

She glanced up quickly at the endearment. He was waiting as if he thought she might actually try to seduce him.

"No," she whispered. She didn't want to play games.

"Ah. Well then, Victoria, my lovely wife, I guess I'll just have to try and seduce you. Tell me if I'm doing this right." And he unbuttoned the top button on his shirt.

Victoria gasped.

He popped the second button.

Her heart began to race out of control. "Why are you doing this?" she asked.

"Because I'm mad for you." He slid the last button

free and started to work on his shirt cuff. "Because I don't want to live without you, but I don't see any way to convince you or get you back, so I'll at least try to get as much of you as you'll let me have. You did the same once, remember?"

She nodded weakly. "Because I wanted to have a baby." But she had already told him earlier that day that she had wanted more than that.

"I'm doing this," Caleb said, "because I can't get enough of you—ever. Because I want to go to heaven and you're the only woman who can take me there. And I'm doing this, my Victoria, because I love you desperately and I don't want to give you a second to think about walking out of my life again. Don't kill me like that again. Please."

She leaned forward, but she stopped, her fingers just an inch from his chest, her lips just a breath away from touching his. "You've dated a lot of women. You've probably told a number of them that you loved them."

He reached out and cupped her chin. He brought his lips even closer. "There were never that many women, Victoria. And there was never ever a woman like you in my life. I've never told another woman I loved her, and you know I don't lie."

Finally, her heart broke free of her doubts. She smiled and launched herself into his arms. "I know you don't lie, Caleb Fremont. And I do love you. I hope you don't mind."

"This is how much I don't mind, love," he told Victoria as he kissed her. "I'm sticking by your side for life. We'll be a family, just you, me and Bob."

"And Lionel, too," she whispered.

"And any other creatures you want to bring home. Bring them all, bring a million, just as long as you keep me, too."

"Always, forever. You're definitely a keeper," she said, and she slipped back into his arms.

Epilogue

Caleb was sitting on the patio, his laptop on the table beside him when Victoria stepped outside, their daughter, Jillie, in her arms.

Immediately he rose to his feet, skirting the table as he moved forward and kissed his daughter and his wife. "Ah, my favorite people in the world. Can I help you?" he asked.

Victoria got a speculative look on her face, a small twinkle in her eyes. "Maybe. Could be. I've been thinking. Could you—that is, I was thinking I might like another baby."

Caleb grinned. "Is this some code phrase?" he asked. "Does this mean the same thing as it did the first time I met you? Are you inviting me to your bed?"

Victoria laughed and bopped him on the arm. "You

are incorrigible. I meant adoption, of course. You know I'm infertile and it doesn't work that way with me."

"Mmm, I know, but it works for me. I would love to have a child, and I'll take any opportunity to get you into my arms."

Victoria arched her brows and raised up and kissed him on the chin. She placed her daughter in her playpen and gave the baby her favorite stuffed parrot. "Jillie's going to want a nap soon. I'll meet you in our room then. Think about what I said." She turned and started to go back into the house.

He caught his wife's hand and kissed the palm slowly, savoring her taste. "There's no need to think."

She sighed. "I really *am* serious, you know. Do you really not mind having another child?"

Caleb slipped his hands around her waist. "Victoria, you and Jillie have brought me the kind of joy I've never known. I'd love to have another child. Maybe several more."

Victoria rose on her toes and looped an arm around his neck. She smiled. "You've changed my life, too. You've taught me to dream. And when you get up to our room today, I'm going to seduce you. This time I'm going to do it right."

A deep laugh escaped him. "Ah, love, didn't you know that you did it right the first time? Exactly right. I was desperate to have you. You made me realize that I was wrong about everything I had ever believed, most definitely about my unwillingness to marry and risk love."

"I'm glad you took the risk," she whispered.

"Me, too. Let's take some more."

"Wanted—one man to love and to love me in return," she whispered, gazing up at him.

He brushed her hair back from her temple and kissed her there. "I'm your man," he told her. And he was.

* * * * *

If you enjoyed what you just read,
then we've got an offer you can't resist!

Take 2 bestselling love stories FREE!
Plus get a FREE surprise gift!

ATHENA FORCE

The Athena Academy adventure continues....

Three secret sisters
Three super talents
One unthinkable legacy...

**The ties that bind may be the ties that kill
as these extraordinary women race against
time to beat the genetic time bomb that is
their birthright....**

**Don't miss the latest three stories
in the Athena Force continuity**

DECEIVED by Carla Cassidy, January 2005

CONTACT by Evelyn Vaughn, February 2005

PAYBACK by Harper Allen, March 2005

**And coming in April–June 2005,
the final showdown for
Athena Academy's best and brightest!**

Available at your favorite retail outlet.